CW00816179

Peppermint's Twist

THE DEVIL'S HANDMAIDENS MC: ATLANTIC CITY, NJ CHAPTER

ANDI RHODES

BLUE JOURNEY PUBLISHING

Also by Andi Rhodes

Broken Rebel Brotherhood

Broken Souls

Broken Innocence

Broken Boundaries

Broken Rebel Brotherhood: Complete Series Box set

Broken Rebel Brotherhood: Next Generation

Broken Hearts

Broken Wings

Broken Mind

Bastards and Badges

Stark Revenge

Slade's Fall

Jett's Guard

Soulless Kings MC

Fender

Joker

Piston

Greaser

Riker

Trainwreck

Squirrel

Gibson

Satan's Legacy MC

Snow's Angel

Toga's Demons

Magic's Torment

Duck's Salvation

Dip's Flame

Devil's Handmaidens MC

Harlow's Gamble

Peppermint's Twist

Mama's Rules

Valhalla Rising MC

Viking

Mayhem Makers

Forever Savage

Prologue

NICO

13 years old…

"I'M SORRY."

I lift my head from the mat on the floor to glare at my twin brother and am not surprised that his expression doesn't match his tone. Nicholi is good at saying what he thinks someone wants to hear, even when it's the furthest thing from the truth. Even at thirteen, he's a master manipulator and our father's favorite son.

"Just leave me alone," I mumble, unable to open my mouth to speak normally.

I hate showing him, or anyone, weakness, but after being beaten by Father, I have no strength left. I am physically and mentally drained.

Nicholi walks further into the small room, only to stop when his toes touch the mat. "You should've listened to Yanni."

Maybe he's right, maybe I should have listened to Father's lead goon. But I couldn't. Not when it meant hurting the prettiest thing I've ever seen since our mother disappeared. I was already on Father's shit list, so what was one more act of defiance?

"He's gonna send you away, ya know?"

There's no mistaking the happiness in Nicholi's tone. He hates me. And if I'm sent away, he'll be the only remaining heir to Father's ridiculous throne. What he forgets though is Father isn't top dog in the Ricci Crime Family. Uncle Antonio holds that honor, which makes our cousins, Malachi and Mortichi, next in line to inherit everything.

When I remain silent, Nicholi kicks me in the ribs. Pain ricochets through my body, zigzagging across my nerves like a lightning bolt in an electrical storm. I wheeze as I try to catch my breath, but I'm unable to inhale much air before he kicks me again. And again and again.

"That's enough!"

Nicholi jumps back at the sound of Father's shout, but not before shooting me an evil smirk. How he and I share the exact same DNA, I'll never know. We're as opposite as night and day, not that it matters.

"Nicholi, Yanni is waiting for you in the car," Father says. "He will drive you home."

"I don't wanna go home."

Father backhands him across the face. "You will do as you are told," he sneers.

Nicholi lowers his head and folds his hands in front of him. "Yes, Father." After a few steps, he turns around and flips me off behind Father's back. Then he disappears out of the room.

Father stalks toward me, and the closer he gets, the darker his expression becomes. "Get up," he commands.

I attempt to roll to my hands and knees, but the pain is too great. Father reaches down and, with a fistful of my hair, yanks my head back to an almost impossible angle.

"I said. Get. Up." Spittle hits my cheek before he shoves

me back down. "You have until the count of five to get on your goddamn feet. Trust me when I say, you don't want me to reach five." Taking a step back, he crosses his arms over his chest. "One."

I try to roll over again, but only end up increasing the agony in my chest.

"Two."

Pain often hinders a person's ability to accomplish a certain goal, like standing up, but where pain lives, fear isn't too far away. The thing about fear is it's a powerful motivator and right now, I need all the motivation I can get.

"Three."

Fearing further punishment, I push myself past the pain and scoot toward the wall. I use the surface as leverage to get up off the floor, but my progress is slow.

"Four."

With the last of my strength, I turn to face my father, while using the wall as support to lean against. I have no doubt the man would prefer me standing on my own, but he didn't specify. Even if he had, I don't think I could.

Father crosses the room in two strides and towers over me. "So you *can* follow instructions."

"Yes, sir," I whisper.

He shakes his head in disgust. "It seems you are forever doomed to be a disappointment. First you hack into highly sensitive files and then you refuse to participate in the very business that puts food on the table and a roof over your head."

Father begins to pace. I remain quiet, knowing that pacing for him is like stretching before you exercise. He's doing something small in order to prepare for something big. "I remember the day you were born, Nico. You and your brother. I was so proud to be the father to not one, but two sons. Two more Ricci boys." He chuckles. "I bragged for months about how you would both grow to be strong, loyal sons. You and Nicholi would carry on the Ricci name, would follow in my and my brother's footsteps." He stops in front of me and glares. "Imagine my surprise when only one of you turned out like me."

"I'm so—"

"I wasn't done," he snarls as he starts to pace again. "Nicholi is a good boy, a loyal son. You, on the other hand, are… not. You are your mother's child. My sweet, *pathetic* Rosetta."

The story Nicholi and I have always been told is that our mother walked out on my father and us because she couldn't handle the lifestyle we were being raised in. But I know the truth. I know my father killed her. Our nanny let it slip one time, after a few too many of her nightly 'sleepy teas' as she called them.

"Rosetta couldn't hack it as a Ricci," Father continues. "And I'm coming to realize, neither can you." Again, he stops in front of me. "So here's what's going to happen. Yanni will be back here shortly with your belongings. He will then drive you to an undisclosed location, where you will be permitted to heal. Once your injuries have healed enough, he'll take you to the airport, where a representative from the Evergreen Boys Academy in Washington state will be waiting."

Is this really happening?

I know I should be frightened, but all I feel is hope. Anything is better than being raised by Father.

"The representative will escort you to the academy, where you will reside, under a new identity, until you turn eighteen. You will no longer go by Nico Ricci. As of this moment, Nico Ricci doesn't exist."

"What?" I blurt, unable to comprehend that bit of information.

"You are dead to me. As far as the world is concerned, I have a son, Nicholi, and he is my *only* son. I do not know what your new identity is, as I want there to be no mistaking that we have zero connection."

This has to be a joke. It all seems too good to be true.

"Do you understand?"

"Yes, sir."

Father heaves a sigh. "It didn't have to be this way, you know? You could have fucked that girl like your brother did. You're never too young to learn about a woman's body, and what better way to practice than on a bitch you'll never see again?"

My stomach rolls at his callous words. Never too young? I'm thirteen! This is why he's doing me a favor by sending me away. I don't want to rape a girl. I don't want to grow up treating others like they're commodities to be bought, sold, traded, and used. I want something more for my life, something better.

I want to become a man my mother would have been proud of. And that's certainly not going to happen under the rule of Angelo Ricci or under the thumb of the Ricci Crime Family.

"Do you have anything you want to say?" Father asks.

I think about it for a moment. My instincts tell me to keep my mouth shut, so as not to incur his wrath. But then I remember he said that I'll be hidden away while my injuries heal. He doesn't want anyone to know about the abuse I've suffered. With that thought in mind, I do something I've never done before.

I say exactly what I want.

"Fuck you."

Father backhands me, getting in one last blow, and I don't even have it in me to care. Being able to utter those two words was worth that extra bite of pain.

CHAPTER 1

Peppermint

PRESENT DAY...

"WHAT'S YOUR NAME?"

I lift my head at the unfamiliar voice, a jolt of hope flashing through my system because it doesn't belong to the man who's been guarding me and the others for the last however many days. I stopped trying to keep track after what was probably only a few hours. Being chained to the floor in a room with no windows and no clocks made it not only extremely difficult but also unbearable to think about.

When I don't answer him, the young boy backhands me across the face. The pain is excruciating, but I do my best to hide it. If I've learned anything since being snatched off the street on my way to school it's that the people who are holding me somehow get worse when any of us react.

"I asked you a question."

He might be younger than the others who've taken to visiting those of us in this hell hole, but his eyes are just as dark and evil. He seems to be around my age, but it's hard to tell under the dim light of the single bulb hanging from the ceiling.

"Can't we just leave her alone?"

That's odd. The boy spoke but his mouth didn't move. I wonder if he's one of those ventr—

"Shut up," he sneers as he throws a look toward the corner of the room.

I follow his gaze and shrink back into the wall when I see there's another boy crouched there. He looks similar to the one who hit me but then again, my mind could be playing tricks on me. Between the drugs and torture, insanity very likely is setting in.

"She's not gonna talk to you, stupid," the one in the corner says.

"Then I'll beat the information out of her like Father or Yanni would."

He leers at me, and if I weren't already at a disadvantage, I might laugh at him. He reminds me of the boys at school, the ones who are mean to the girls when they like them. Idiots. I flinch when his hand rests on my bare leg, and when he glides it up over my knee toward my exposed privates, I whimper.

"You don't have to be like them," Corner Boy comments quietly.

I curl in on myself when the one in front of me lunges toward the corner. The chain around my ankle rattles, giving away the fear I'm trying so hard to hide. Squeezing my eyes shut, I block out the sounds of their fighting and force my mind to go to another place. I've gotten pretty good at this trick recently.

I'm not able to pretend for long though, because a rough hand on my leg pulls me back to reality. I don't know which of the two boys the hand belongs to, but if the cold calculation in the eyes is anything to go by, it's the one who was tormenting me to begin with.

Turning my head, I command my body not to react to the sharp bite of his teeth on my skin or the way his fingers dig into the flesh of my thighs as he shoves my legs apart. Air gets trapped in my lungs when he grips my chin and forces me to look at him. How can someone so young be so cruel?

"I listen to the screams when Yanni is in here playing with all of you," he taunts as he kneels between my spread knees, nodding toward the other captives. "At first, I worried because Father told me that the buyers he has lined up want you all untouched." He *shrugs. "But I don't have to worry anymore because we were instructed to do this."*

The boy fumbles with the button on his pants. His hands are shaking, which is a stark contrast to the confidence he's portraying. I watch in horror as he lowers his zipper and straightens to push his jeans down.

I bolt up from the mattress before shoving the blanket off my legs to rush to the attached bathroom. As I drop to my knees in front of the toilet, my stomach heaves up its contents. Sweat pours down my back, and my muscles tense with each spasm.

When there's nothing left for my body to expel, I drop back to my ass and lean against the wall. I yank the towel from the rack above my head and use it to wipe my face off. I'm exhausted, both physically and mentally.

My nightmares are nothing new. I had them for months after I was taken as a teenager, but I thought I had things under control. I'd gone years without them. Fucking years. But then Malachi Ricci came along and shook shit up.

Once I'm reasonably certain I can move without praying to the porcelain god again, I rise to my feet and move to the sink to brush my teeth. My reflection taunts me from the mirror, so I close my eyes, but that only makes things worse because images from my nightmares dance behind my lids.

"Goddamn Ricci's," I mutter.

I drop my toothbrush in the little cup next to the faucet and make my way back into my bedroom. My cell phone lights up from the nightstand as the alarm goes off. The high-pitched sound wreaks havoc on my head, and I quickly silence it.

Coffee. I need copious amounts of coffee before I can even think about heading downstairs to the main level of the club-house. As the Vice President of the Devil's Handmaidens MC: Atlantic City, NJ chapter, I'm permitted to live off-site, but since it's just me, I don't really see the point in spending the money on rent or a mortgage when I don't have to. My room here suits me just fine.

While my Keurig brews my liquid energy, my mind wanders to the family that forced my demons to the surface: the Ricci's. Malachi Ricci is engaged to Harlow, my best friend and president of the DHMC, so I've learned to love and respect him. He also helped us take out his family's entire human trafficking organization, so there's that. It's hard to hate a man who hates the same things and people I do.

Unfortunately, taking out the organization didn't result in eliminating the entire Ricci clan. Malachi's cousin, Nicholi, got away, and we've spent the last year trying to find him. And then there's Nico Ricci, Malachi's other cousin and Nicholi's twin brother.

As I lift the full mug to my lips, my cell phone dings with a notification. I ignore it until the mug is empty and I've got a second one brewing.

"Speak of the devil," I mumble when I look at the phone screen.

Nico: Morning.

I roll my eyes but can't stop the corner of my mouth from lifting slightly. Nico is… complicated. It's a love hate sorta thing. Well, that's not entirely accurate. It's more of a tolerate hate sorta thing.

Nico is Malachi's partner at Forza Security, the security firm they started, and the head of the team that tracks Nicholi. Not that we've gotten anywhere with that. He's also the man who asked me to marry him and have his babies the very first time we talked. And no amount of threatening bodily harm has slowed him down in his pursuit.

My phone dings again as I traipse down the stairs to the main floor.

Nico: What? Not even a threat this morning?

Pausing on the step, I type out a quick response.

Me: Fuck off

I tuck the phone in the pocket of my green joggers and ignore my notifications. If Nico wants to play this game, he needs to grow some balls and show his face in Atlantic City. As it stands, he's refused to come back, even though his father, and the rest of the Ricci Crime Family, is gone.

"Hey, Pep."

I smile at Fiona, a newly patched member, and slide onto an empty stool at the bar. "Please tell me you made some pancakes before you started inventory."

Fiona chuckles. "You're lucky Coast got called out in the middle of the night, otherwise I'd have made them at home for him."

I've never been so happy that she's married to a cop. Fortunately, Coast understands MC life, as he's the VP of his club. While it's unconventional to have a patched member who's married to law enforcement, it's worked out in our favor on more than one occasion.

"Here ya go," Fiona says as she slides a plate full of pancakes in front of me.

"You're an angel."

Fiona returns to doing inventory while I dig into my food. I just put the last bite into my mouth when the door to the clubhouse slams open. I whirl around to see Harlow and Malachi striding toward me with matching angry expressions.

"What's up?" I ask as I hop off my stool.

Harlow lifts her gaze to look at Malachi and he nods slightly. When she returns her attention to me, I mentally brace myself for whatever bomb she's about to drop.

"We've got trouble."

CHAPTER 2

Nico

"ANYTHING ELSE, SIR?"

I force a smile at my assistant, Bethany, and hope like hell she doesn't notice the way my eye twitches at her use of the title. I may be her boss, but I can't stand the formality that society dictates should come with the position. This is why I insisted on running the Seattle branch of Forza Security from my home and not a stuffy office building. I also refuse to wear a suit and tie, as I much prefer jeans and whatever shirt is clean on any given morning, but that's beside the point.

"Nope." I smirk when Bethany fails to hide her disapproval of my casual attitude. Apparently, no one taught her that it's rude to roll your eyes at the person who signs your paychecks. I'd call her on it if I didn't find it so amusing. "Why don't you head home? Those reports can wait until Monday."

Bethany glances down at her notebook, no doubt mentally calculating how long it will take her to type the notes I dictated to her into the system. Seemingly satisfied that it won't take too much of her time, she offers a polite smile.

"Are you sure? I don't mind sta—"

I hold a hand up. "I'm sure, Bethany. I've already kept you late enough."

She stands from her chair and holds her notebook to her chest. "Thank you, sir. Have a good weekend," she quips before darting out the door.

If she only knew.

I haven't had a good weekend in I don't fucking know how long, and this weekend isn't going to be any different. Unlike Bethany, I can't walk out the door and turn the work off at the end of the day because I've got one case that never stops: my piece of shit twin brother.

Nicholi and I were forced to travel two very different roads in life. I was shipped off to boarding school, exiled from the Family and deemed not good enough. Nicholi was embraced by the Family, groomed and taught to be the brutal man he is today.

I had no contact with my biological family until years after being sent away, when my uncle killed my cousin's girlfriend. At the time, I didn't know how Malachi would receive me, but I didn't care. I had information and he had a reason to act on it. Together, and with the help of his now fiancé's motorcycle club, we ended our family's reign of terror.

Oh, and in the process, I met the love of my life. I use the word 'met' loosely because we've never actually been face to face, but that doesn't seem to matter. The moment I heard her voice as she was reading me, Malachi, and her club the riot act, I was a goner. Too bad she doesn't feel the same.

I lift my cell off my desk and open the texting app to see if I've missed any messages from Peppermint. I know I haven't, but I can't stop myself from checking anyway. It's become a part of my daily routine, right along with my 'Morning' texts to her. I don't even mind the 'fuck off' responses because at least she's acknowledging me.

Now that Bethany is gone, I decide to switch to my laptop and get out of my home office for a while. I grab everything I'll need to do my nightly dive into tracking Nicholi and carry it all into the living room of my penthouse apartment.

After dropping it all onto the couch, I start toward the kitchen, but a knock on the door slows me down.

"Come in," I yell, thinking maybe Bethany forgot something.

"You own fifty percent of a security firm, and you don't even check to see who's at the door before inviting them in?"

I whirl around with wide eyes and stare at a man I haven't seen since we were kids. My cousin grins.

"What are… Are you… I can't…" I shake my head to clear it and then close the distance between us and throw my arms around his neck. "Damn, man, it's been a long time."

Malachi hugs me back, both of us holding on tight. After what some would probably deem too long, I slap him on the back and step away.

"What are you doing here?"

"Do I need a reason to pop in and see you?"

"Nothing about this is you just popping in," I deadpan. "You live in New Jersey for fuck's sake."

"So?"

"So, you're here in Seattle."

Malachi follows me into the kitchen. I grab two tumblers and the bottle of whiskey from the cupboard. After pouring both of us a drink, I slide his across the island to him and down mine in one gulp.

"So?" I prod as I pour myself another. "It's not a difficult question, man. What brings you here?"

He heaves a sigh. "The answer is a little more difficult than the question itself."

"Well that's cryptic as fuck."

Malachi's expression darkens. "We need you to come back to Atlantic City."

Before I can react or respond, his cell phone rings. He

pulls it out of his pocket and taps the screen to answer it on speakerphone.

"Is he coming back with you?" Harlow asks before Malachi can say a word.

"*He* can hear you, Harlow," I bite out, although I'm not mad. I like Harlow's no-nonsense attitude and have since the first time we spoke.

"Good. Then listen closely," she snaps. "You're gonna pack some shit and come back with Malachi. You're needed here, not holed up in your penthouse apartment with your ass parked in front of your computers."

Malachi coughs, but he fails to hide his laugh.

"What's so funny?" she demands.

"Nothing, *bella*," Malachi soothes. "It's just, Nico hasn't exactly said no."

"I haven't said yes either," I remind him.

"You will," Harlow insists. "Once you have all the facts, you won't be able to stay away."

"You're awfully sure of—" My brain registers all her words. "Wait, what facts?"

I stare at Malachi, and he stares at the phone. When Harlow doesn't explain, my cousin lifts his gaze to me and sighs. "He's back."

I clench my jaw at that bit of information. "How do you know?"

"Because all the signs point to Nicholi being in Atlantic City and picking up right where the *family* left off."

"What signs?"

"People are disappearing off the streets, several bodies have turned up."

"That's not unique to Nicholi."

"No, but the drugs that turned up on the toxicology reports are unique to the Ricci's old… *enterprises*."

My mind flashes to the shit my father and uncle had created to keep their merchandise cooperative. A shiver races through me when I imagine how many people had that concoction pumped through their veins... me included.

"Nico?" Malachi prompts. "You okay? You're lookin' a little pale."

Malachi doesn't know about that though. No one does. And he doesn't need to know. Not right now anyway.

I wave away his concern. "I'm fine."

"So you'll come back with Malachi?" Harlow asks.

As hard as it will be, there is no other option. I need to be a part of taking out Nicholi just as much as they do. Maybe more so.

"Yeah, I'll come back with him."

"Seriously?" Malachi asks.

"Did you honestly think I was going to say no?"

"I wasn't sure, to be honest," he admits. "You've stayed away for the last year so..." He shrugs as he lets his words trail off.

"Motherfucker!"

My eyes snap to the phone at the sound of Peppermint, my favorite spitfire. How she's kept her mouth shut this entire conversation, I'll never know. She typically jumps at the chance to argue with me.

"Ah, *cuore mio.* I didn't know you were on the line."

Peppermint groans. "How many times do I have to tell you to stop calling me your heart?"

"I'll never stop."

"Har, I swear I'm gonna kill him when he gets here."

"Don't listen to her, Nico," Malachi says with a chuckle. "She's just mad because she owes me a hundred bucks."

I narrow my eyes at him. "You didn't?"

Malachi's grin widens. "I did."

I tsk. "Oh, *cuore mio,* you should never bet against a Ricci."

"Fuck you."

I smile as I imagine her stomping around the room throwing an adult-sized temper tantrum.

"You will… soon."

"Jesus, my ears are gonna start bleeding," Harlow grumbles. "Can we please get back to the reason I'm not getting fucked for the next few days?"

Both Malachi and I burst out laughing. Talk about bleeding ears.

Once I catch my breath, I look at my cousin. "So, when do we leave?"

CHAPTER 3

Peppermint

"IS it just me or do they keep getting younger?"

The basement of Devil's Double Down casino used to bring a sense of accomplishment, but lately, it only serves as a reminder that we're fighting a losing battle. It won't stop the Devil's Handmaidens from staying in the war though. Nothing will stop us.

"Does it matter?" I counter. "They're all still victims."

Human trafficking runs rampant in our city. And it's getting worse by the day now that Nicholi Ricci is back in the game.

Harlow sighs and shakes her head. "No, I guess it doesn't."

As we stand there and observe a few other members taking care of the ten girls we rescued today, my stomach balls into knots. All ten have needle marks on their necks, and all ten were out of it when we stormed the rundown shack where they were being held… just like I was.

As if my nightmares weren't bad enough, now I have to deal with the similarities to my own kidnapping in the light of day.

"Are you okay?" Harlow asks as she wraps an arm around my shoulder.

She's not normally a touchy-feely kinda girl so I can imagine that her actions speak volumes about my demeanor.

I nod slowly. "Yeah, I'll be fine."

"You're a terrible liar."

And because she's right, I pull away from her and weave through several empty cots toward a girl who appears to be waking up. I watch as her eyes flutter open, and the look of panic that crosses her features tugs on my heartstrings to the point of snapping. I know that look, that feeling. I know it well.

When the girl tries to sit up, I rush forward to steady her, but she jerks away from me so hard she falls off the other side. Rage crashes over me like a tidal wave. What the hell did she endure for her to be so scared?

You know exactly what she went through.

I slowly walk around the cot, taking deep breaths as I do, and crouch down beside her. "You're safe here," I say gently.

The girl shifts to a sitting position and pulls her knees tightly to her chest. She keeps her head lowered, but there's no missing the tears that are streaming down her dirty cheeks. The streaks in the wake of the salty drops leave her face looking a little wild.

"I wanna go home," she manages to push out between her sobs.

I rest my hand on her shoulder, keeping it there when she flinches. Trust is earned, and I have to prove to her that she can trust me, trust the club. That won't happen if I back off every time she shows fear.

"I'm not gonna hurt you."

Several minutes pass, and I remain silent while she works hard to slow her crying. When it subsides into wet hiccups, she lifts her head and looks at me. I force a smile in an effort to help her stay calm.

"Can you tell me your name?" I ask.

"Sara."

"Hi Sara. I'm Peppermint."

Sara scrunches her nose. "Like the candy?"

"Yeah, like the candy."

"That's a weird name."

I chuckle. "I guess it is."

Sara darts her gaze around the room. "Where are we?"

Now that she's talking, I lower my hand and shift to sit on my ass. Sara scoots a few inches away before turning to face me fully.

"Someplace safe." I tilt my head. "How old are you, Sara?"

"Nine." She sniffles.

I consciously make an effort not to react to that. So fucking young. She probably still believed the world was full of unicorns and rainbows before she was taken. She won't believe anymore though. Her world will forever be tainted with evil, even if she works past it and thinks she's moved on. The evil will lurk, in the shadows of her mind and soul, and it will pounce when she least expects it.

Trust me, I would know.

Sara's eyelids begin to droop. Her adrenaline is finally waning, exhaustion taking its place.

"Why don't you try to get some rest?" I suggest. When she nods, I extend a hand to help her up and then cover her with the blanket after she settles on the cot. "Sara, do you know your phone number so I can call your parents?"

Sara yawns but manages to rattle off a number. I pull my cell out and store the number in my contacts before shoving the phone back into my pocket. As Sara drifts to sleep, I stride to the door and step outside, inhaling the fresh air as soon as the sun hits my face.

The click of the automatic lock engaging is like a tripwire on my fury. Whirling around, I slam my fist into the concrete wall. Pain spreads through my knuckles but I ignore it as I punch the wall, over and over and over again. I don't stop until the sound of the door opening breaks through the haze of my anger.

"Feel better?"

I glance to my left and see Tahiti leaning against the wall with her arms crossed over her chest. We stare at each other, me with my chest heaving and her as calm as can be. She doesn't push me to answer, just waits me out until I can't stand the silence any longer.

"Sure."

Tahiti lowers her gaze to my hands, which are hanging at my sides. "You're gonna need to get those looked at."

I lift my hands in front of my face and take in the blood dripping from my split skin. "I'll be fine."

"Let me rephrase that," she says as she pushes away from the wall. "You will get those looked at."

Her tone demands obedience, which only spurs my temper. I square my shoulders. "Last time I checked, I outrank you. Remember that."

"You're right." Tahiti shrugs. "But you and I both know you'll listen because you don't want to incite Harlow's wrath, which is inevitable if you do nothing and get an infection."

What is it with everyone being right about shit today?

"Dammit, you're annoying."

"Only because I care."

"I know, T. And I appreciate it."

"Good." She shoves her hands in her pockets. "Now, why were you trying to maul the building?"

I snort. "Like you don't know."

"Tell me anyway," she prods.

I take a deep breath and exhale loudly. "It never ends."

"What?"

"The pain, the injustice, the constant stream of victims, the never-ending influx of monsters, the memories, the night-mares... Take your fucking pick."

"If the missions are too much, just talk to—"

"They're not," I snap. "I needed a minute, that's all."

Tahiti holds her hands up. "If you say so." She turns and presses her palm against the scanner by the door. When the lock disengages, she pulls the door open. "Harlow wanted me to let you know she was heading to the clubhouse and would see you there later."

"Thanks." I take out my cell, not bothering to worry about the blood smearing on the screen. "I've got a call to make."

Tahiti nods and then disappears inside.

Once alone, I tap on the number Sara gave me and press the phone to my ear. After the fourth ring, a woman answers.

"Hello?"

"Hi. You don't know me, but I got your number from Sara. Are you—"

"Is this some sort of sick joke?" the woman demands, anguish lacing her words.

"No, ma'am, it's not a joke. Are you Sara's mother?"

"We both know I am," she snaps. "And you are?"

"My name is Pepper, but my friends call me Peppermint. I'm calling to let you know that Sara is safe."

It takes another twenty minutes and a chat with Sara for Sue—she finally told me her name—to believe that this isn't a joke, and that Sara is alive and well. Sara was abducted from her birthday party, a little over a month ago, which was held at a local skating rink in her hometown just outside of Little Rock, Arkansas. Her parents are driving all night so they can pick her up tomorrow.

Satisfied that at least one of the victims we rescued today will get some semblance of her life back, I make my way to the corner where the doc has his supplies set up. Nathan Claymore is officially employed by Malachi and Nico, but he always helps us out when summoned.

"Hey, Pep," Nathan says. He nods at my hands. "Need me to take a look?"

"Please."

"Sure thing. Have a seat and I'll stitch you up as soon as I finish with the last girl."

"Thanks, Nate."

He walks over to the girl two cots over from Sara. The girl flinches and jerks away from him at first, much like Sara did, but he quickly and efficiently gets an IV hooked up and the sedative he always has on hand calms her so he can work.

While I wait, I close my eyes. It's been a long day, and I'm beat. I want nothing more than to go to the clubhouse, climb the stairs to my room, and lock myself inside to collapse on the bed.

Unfortunately, that won't be possible because once Nate's finished with me, I have nine more victims to talk to and nine more families to notify.

Like I told Tahiti… never-fucking-ending.

CHAPTER 4

Nico

"HOW'S IT FEEL?"

I shift my gaze from the passenger window to Malachi. The last few days have been a whirlwind, to say the least, but he's been fairly relaxed through it all. Now, though, my cousin seems tense. His knuckles are white from gripping the steering wheel, and his back is ramrod straight.

"How does what feel?"

Malachi spares me a glance. "Don't play dumb. You know what I mean."

He's right, I do. I'm just not at all sure how to answer him. I decide on honesty because let's face it, neither of us has had a ton of that in our lives.

I shrug. "I don't think it's quite set in yet."

"It will. This is the first time you've been in the city in what? Ten years?"

"Eleven," I correct. "But who's counting?"

"Right."

Silence fills the vehicle as Malachi focuses on driving, and I return to staring out the window. I expected to recognize my surroundings but so far, I haven't. And that only adds to my unease. If nothing is familiar, how can I tell when something is going to have a negative effect on me? The thought is unsettling, to say the least.

I'm so lost in my own head that I don't even realize that Malachi has turned off the main road until he stops the car next to a guard shack and rolls down his window.

"Hey, Malachi." The woman steps out of the shack and leans in to look at me. "Who ya got there?"

"Vinnie, this is my cousin, Nico," Malachi says. "Nico, meet Vinnie. She's a DHMC prospect."

"I've heard a lot about ya, but it's nice to meet you anyway."

Malachi laughs. "Get back to work, Vinnie. He doesn't need to hear about how much Peppermint bitches about him."

Ignoring the line of conversation I really want to pursue, I focus on Vinnie. "Nice to meet you too."

When she steps back from the car, Malachi rolls his window up and proceeds to drive through the gate. I want to take in my surroundings, familiarize myself with every inch of the place, but I can't take my eyes off Malachi and his smug expression.

"Seriously?"

"What?" he asks, feigning innocence.

"Does she really bitch about me that much?"

"Put it this way," he begins. "Everyone knows she'd as soon slice off your balls than have a conversation with you."

My hands immediately cup my junk and Malachi laughs. He parks the car in front of a cinderblock building. I recognize it from photos, but it's even more impressive in person. I lean forward to get a better look out the windshield.

"It's not much to look at, but it's a fortress." He shakes his head. "It wasn't always that way, though. Did I tell you about the first time I came here?"

I sit back and chuckle. "Yeah, about a hundred times."

"Yeah, sorry about that."

"No, you're not," I joke. "And it's okay. I'm glad you found Harlow. I'm glad you're happy."

"I really am," he confirms with a wide grin. "I'd be even happier if Nicholi were dead, but we'll get there."

"You and me both."

As I follow Malachi inside, I scan the row of motorcycles pulled up to the building. I recognize Peppermint's Harley immediately. It's all black except for the gas tank, which is painted to look like, well, a peppermint, with red and white stripes.

When we step inside, I take in the large black room. There's a logo painted on the floor, as well as behind the bar that's situated along one wall. Several tables and couches are spread throughout the space, and there's a large flat screen television mounted on the wall. The ambiance is rounded out with a pool table and some dart boards.

I don't know what I expected as far as a crowd goes, but it certainly isn't what's in front of me. Besides Malachi and me, there are only five other people here, all of them women. Harlow is easy to spot because she's currently rushing toward us with her sights set on Malachi.

Ignoring them, I lock my gaze on the only other person in the room I care about. Peppermint is currently dancing in the middle of the floor, her body moving to the beat of some rock song I couldn't care less about. And my cock is rigid at the sight of her.

"Don't let her catch you doing that."

I pull my attention away from Peppermint to look at the woman standing on my left. She's wearing a smirk and her eyes are fixated on my hand which is not so subtly adjusting my jeans.

When she lifts her gaze, her smirk turns into a full-blown smile. "I'm Giggles." She holds out her hand for me to shake, which I do. "You must be Nico."

"That's me," I confirm but my focus is already returning to Peppermint.

"Yeah, you're fucked." Giggles pats me on the back and walks away.

How is it that a woman I barely know can have such a pull on me? She hasn't even noticed me, and it still feels like we're the only two people in the room, like she's dancing just for me.

I watch her for a few more minutes, mentally gearing up to go say 'hi', but before I can move, a small hand grips my forearm. I turn to my right and see Harlow and Malachi standing next to me.

"Thank you for coming," Harlow says as she rises to her tiptoes to wrap her arms around my neck.

I return her hug and a strange sensation settles in my chest. It's one thing to know someone over the phone, but it's another when they're right there in front of you. I've grown to love Harlow over the last year, like I imagine I'd love a sister. Definitely more than I loved my brother.

"Not much would have kept me away."

Harlow steps back, but her hands remain on my arms. And based on the way Malachi is murdering me with his glare, he's not thrilled about it.

"You can stop touching him now," he growls, tugging her into his side.

Harlow's hand immediately goes to the hatchet I've heard so much about. "And you can stop being so jealous," she bites out. "He's family, and I'll touch family if I want to touch family."

"Like fuck you will," Malachi snaps.

"Seriously?" Harlow steps out of his hold and unsheathes her hatchet. Her expression shifts from annoyed to heated in the blink of an eye as she holds the blade to his neck. "Does someone need me to show him how much I want his cock and only his cock?"

"Always."

There are no words for how sickening they are together…
and how jealous I am of them.

Malachi tugs Harlow toward the stairs, but Harlow digs in
her heels. "We'll disappear in a minute," she tells him. "Let
me make sure Peppermint doesn't kill Nico and then I'm all
yours."

"Do not piss her off," Malachi demands of me with a
glare.

I hold my hands up innocently. "I don't plan on it."

"You don't have to plan shit. You breathe and she's
pissed."

I glance at Peppermint, who's still dancing alone, obliv-
ious to everything and everyone. That is until Harlow goes to
the stereo system and cuts the music. Peppermint notices that.

"Fucking bitch," Peppermint sneers as she stomps
toward us.

Her steps are slightly wobbly, and I can't stop myself
from rushing forward to try and steady her. The second my
hand touches her arm, she flails away from me. I glance at
Harlow to see what her reaction is, but she's only standing
there with her hatchet still in her hand and a scowl on her
face.

"Why'd you shut that off?" Peppermint asks.

"It got your attention, didn't it?" Harlow counters.

Peppermint throws her arms up. "Fine, here I am.
Whaddya want?"

"Pep, you are so goddamn lucky you're my best friend
because otherwise, I'd slice you up for disrespecting me."

"Nah, you wouldn't do that." Peppermint's attention
shifts to Malachi. "Mal! You made it. Welcome to my party."

My cousin shakes his head and chuckles. "Some party."

She scrunches her nose, and the action transforms her
from sexy to adorable. "Well, it's all I got. We only saved ten
today, Mal." Peppermint shakes her head like that's a pitiful

number. "Only ten. And the youngest was nine, Mal. Nine fucking years old."

Malachi nods. "I know. Har filled us in."

"Us?"

Malachi shifts his gaze from her to me, and her eyes follow his. When her stare lands on me, she squints.

"Who're you?"

A normal person would simply respond with their name, but I'm far from normal. I'm a fucking Ricci, whatever the hell that means anymore.

I close the distance between us and lean in to whisper in Peppermint's ear.

"Hi, *cuore mio.*"

She rears back and after blinking several times, her face drains of all color and her entire body goes rigid. The drunk woman from two seconds ago disappears. In her place is a crazed bundle of fury.

She strikes out with a right hook, catching me on the cheek. That's followed up with a left uppercut to the jaw and a knee to the groin.

"Why are you here?" she shouts. "What do you want from me?"

A blade is pressed against my chin, forcing me to straighten from her blitz attack. "Fucking answer me!"

"Pep!" Harlow yells. "Stop it, now!"

She doesn't stop. She slices her blade down my chest, ripping my shirt, but somehow barely breaking the skin. I grab her wrist and twist it enough that she drops the knife, but another knee to my groin and I'm on the floor.

Peppermint drops on top of me, fists flying, rage filled hate spewing from her mouth. I can't make sense of any of it, because all my focus is on protecting myself from her wrath.

What the fuck is happening?

With my arms in front of my face, I block blow after blow until her weight is lifted off me.

"Let me go!" she screams. "I'm gonna kill him. I need to kill him."

A sickening crack reaches my ears through her screams, and I look over just in time to see Peppermint fall to the floor next to me, Malachi's arms around her to ease her fall.

"Tahiti, call the doc and get him here," Harlow says, and that's when I notice that we're surrounded by the other women in the room. She's also shaking her hand out, so I assume it was her who hit Peppermint. "Giggles, sit with her and make sure that she doesn't get up if she comes to."

Harlow moves from her VP to me, her glare sparking fire. "What the fuck was that all about?"

Sitting up, I wince at the pain. "I have no fucking clue."

"Bullshit," she snaps. "Peppermint can be unhinged, sure, but no more than the rest of us and *never* toward someone who doesn't deserve it."

"*Bella*," Malachi says, warning in his tone.

"Don't you dare 'bella' me," she seethes. "You saw what just happened."

"I did, so I know that Nico didn't do anything to provoke her."

"Goddammit!" Harlow jumps to her feet and starts to pace. "Fox, go get him some ice for his face." The woman scrambles to do her bidding. "Fiona, pour us all a drink. I think we could use it."

When Fiona returns, she's balancing a tray of shot glasses full to the brim. I get to my feet and down three in quick succession. The tequila burns a path on the way down, but I savor it.

"Doc said he's twenty minutes out," Tahiti informs Harlow when she returns. "He was staying at the casino tonight in case any of today's rescued needed anything."

"Thanks." Harlow heaves a sigh as she stares down at her best friend, who remains knocked out cold on the floor. "Everyone get outta here. Shut the place down and go to your rooms or head home. I don't care which. Just… fucking go."

Tahiti, Fiona, Fox, and Giggles split up the tasks of shutting down the clubhouse and locking up for the night. Malachi, Harlow, and I remain in place until they're all gone.

"We're not going home, are we?" Malachi asks.

"Not a chance in hell," Harlow replies. "I'm not leaving until I know what set her off."

"I did," I say quietly.

"No shit," Malachi quips. "But why?"

Peppermint stirs but doesn't wake. I crouch down beside her, needing to be close. Reaching out, I brush a strand of hair out of her face, and gently run a finger over her cheek, careful not to touch the split skin from Harlow's fist. And when she leans into my touch, my heart skips a beat.

Without giving it a second thought, I scoop her up in my arms and hold her against my chest as I stand.

"What are you doing?" Malachi asks.

I keep my eyes focused on Peppermint's face. Nothing will make me put her down, but I'm very aware of the damage she can inflict if she wakes up while I'm holding her.

"Where's her room?" Malachi and Harlow exchange a look, so I try again. "Look, I'm not gonna let her lie on the cold floor when she's got a bed somewhere around here. Now, where. Is. Her. Room?"

Harlow sighs. "Follow me."

I carry Peppermint upstairs to the room Harlow leads me to. After laying her on the mattress, I carefully remove her boots and drop them on the floor. Next, I unstrap the empty sheath at her ankle and place it on the nightstand.

"She's gonna want her knife," I say absently.

"I'll get it."

Malachi rushes out of the room, but it's no more than a minute before he returns and puts the hunting knife in its sheath.

"Nico, why are you doing this?" he asks me quietly.

I take a few deep breaths as I process the answer. How can I explain to him what I don't understand myself?

"Nico?" Harlow prompts.

"I'm doing it because I have to."

CHAPTER 5
Peppermint

"TIME TO GO BOYS!"

I recognize Yanni's booming voice a split second before he rushes into the room. The sound of gunfire echoes in the air and an entirely new fear weaves its way through my veins. Yanni grabs the boy from between my legs and shoves a bag in his hands.

"Here, help me dose 'em," he orders.

The boy takes the bag, and my eyes widen when he pulls out several syringes. "In the neck, right?" he asks Yanni.

"Just like I showed you last time."

When the boy takes one of the syringes and bends toward me, Yanni uses his arm to stop him. "She's mine." He nods toward the others. "You get them on your way to the tunnel. Your father is waiting for you there." The boy hesitates so Yanni barks, "Go!"

"I'm sorry, Pep."

The voice booming in my ear no longer belongs to Yanni, but to someone I trust. Which makes this whole situation worse. I attempt to move my hands, to reach out and grab Nate so I can stop him from emptying his needle into my body, but my efforts are useless.

"It's just a mild sedative," Nate says. "To help you relax and remain calm."

I don't want to relax, and fuck being calm. You're keeping me in the dark where my nightmares live. I hate nightmares, especially the one you're sending me back to.

Yanni swings his gaze around the room as if frantically searching for something, and when it lands on the other boy huddled in the corner, he shakes his head.

"Maybe now your father will listen to me when I tell him you're worthless," he mutters as he yanks the boy to his feet and slaps his face until he wakes up.

It takes Corner Boy a second or two to focus, but when he does, Yanni presses a syringe into his hand.

"Dose her," Yanni demands, his voice as sharp as a whip. Corner Boy shakes his head and Yanni backhands him across the face. "You will do as you're told, Boy," he seethes.

When Corner Boy refuses, Yanni wraps a meaty hand around the back of his neck and forces him down toward me. I squeeze my eyes shut and curl in on myself as much as the chains allow, praying it will stop whatever is about to happen. It doesn't.

"I'm sorry."

The fear-laced words are whispered in my ear a second before a rush of cold liquid flows through my veins. I try to open my eyes, to fight the invisible force holding me in darkness, but it's useless.

"That should do it."

I roll away from the sound of Nate's voice but regret it immediately when the pillow aggravates whatever wound is on my cheek. Strong hands urge me to my back, and I find myself being drawn to the touch, like it's a soothing balm for all my anguish.

"You're gonna have to take it easy for a while, *cuore mio.*"

The balm morphs into napalm, and my eyes fly open. I lock eyes with the man leaning over me. I always knew this day would come, the day when I'd be face to face with one of my tormentors. I just never dreamed it would be *him*.

"You were there," I accuse, taking in the bruises on his face.

I did that. I recognized him and fought. But I didn't win.

"Where, Pep?" Harlow asks as she steps closer to the bed. "Where was Nico?"

I roll my neck to face her. "Why did you stop me?" I ask, my voice thick with emotion. "Why didn't you let me kill him?"

Harlow's gaze darts from me to Nico and back again. "Give me a good reason why I shouldn't have stopped you."

I swallow past the lump in my throat. "Because Har, he was there." I close my eyes against the memory, against the wave of nausea it brings. "The day your mom rescued me, Nico was the one who drugged me."

Nico stumbles back, his eyes wide. "No." He shakes his head and repeats that one word. "No. No, no, no."

"Get him outta here," Harlow barks.

Malachi moves from his position by the door and grips Nico's shoulders to guide him out.

"I didn't hurt her," Nico cries. "I swear I didn't."

Malachi kicks the door shut once they cross the threshold, but it doesn't drown out Nico's protests. I do my best to ignore his voice, but even if I could in reality, in my memories, it's always there.

I'm sorry.

Hi, cuore mio.

Harlow sits on the edge of the bed and lifts my hand into her lap. She glances at Nate, who's still standing to the side and looking very uncomfortable.

"Nate, are you finished?" she asks him.

"Uh, yeah," he responds distractedly. He begins to pack up his supplies as he addresses me. "Pep, you might feel drowsy for another twelve hours or so. The sedative won't be completely out of your system, even though it's not keeping you asleep. Your cheek will heal on its own, but it's gonna hurt like a son of a bitch so I'm leaving you some pain meds.

As for your hands, I restitched the cuts from earlier. The swelling will go down in a few days."

"Thanks, doc."

"Anytime."

Nate grabs his jacket off the chair in the corner on his way out, leaving Harlow and I alone. Usually, I can read her like an open book, but at the moment, she's as closed off as a nun's cunt.

"What?" I ask after a few minutes of awkward silence.

"You know I love you, right?"

"Cold-cocking me is a helluva way to show it," I gripe.

"What the fuck was I supposed to do, P? You were losing your shit, and nothing was stopping you. I had to do something."

Unable to stand the concern wrinkling her forehead, I glance away. I brace my hands on the mattress and, ignoring the agony, push myself into a sitting position. Silently, Harlow helps me scoot back to lean against the headboard.

"I know you love me," I finally concede. "Hell, even when you couldn't say the words, I knew."

"Then I need you to listen to me." Harlow tips her head back and rolls the tension from her neck. "I know your story, Pep. Most of it anyway. I've always suspected there's more to it than what you've told me, and I've let you keep it to yourself. Everyone has secrets, right?" She shrugs like it's no big deal. "But no more. What happened downstairs can't happen again."

Annoyance flares. "I can't believe you're taking his side."

"I'm taking your side, P," she snaps. "I will *always* take your side. But letting you deal with your past on your own isn't working."

"What do you want from me?"

"I want you to talk to me." Harlow shakes her head. "No, scratch that. You're going to talk to me. I need to know everything, P. No more secrets."

"There's nothing to—"

"Don't," she barks. "I've put up with secrets, but I've never been okay with lies."

Heaving a sigh, I shift my gaze to stare at the wall. Harlow has never given me a reason to be afraid of how she'll handle the details of my past, but I've never tested her resolve as much as I'm about to.

"I don't even know where to start," I mumble.

Harlow moves to sit next to me on the bed, her side pressed against mine in a silent show of support.

"Start at the beginning."

CHAPTER 6
Nico

"WHY DIDN'T you ever tell me?"

I wince as Nate threads the needle through my flesh. It wasn't until Malachi pressed against my chest to keep me from going back into the bedroom that I even noticed Peppermint had cut deeper than I thought. Deep enough to need stitches.

"What was I supposed to say?" I counter. "I didn't even know who the girl was."

While Nate stitched me up, I explained to Malachi what I could remember about the girl my father wanted me to rape, the girl Yanni forced me to drug.

No, not the *girl. It was Peppermint. How the fuck did I miss that?*

Malachi paces back and forth in the hallway. Nate tried to get me into another room before he started working, but I refused. I didn't want to be too far in case Peppermint needed me.

Keep dreaming dumbass.

"All finished," Nate says as he flattens a bandage across the freshly stitched wound. "Try not to get in the way of any more knives."

"Doc, you've met the women in this club," Malachi jokes. "Hatchets, axes, and knives are like toys to them."

"And toys can still do damage." Nate raises a brow. "Or are you forgetting the stitches I had to give you a couple months ago when Harlow got a little too... excited?"

My head whips to the side to take in the flush that creeps up Malachi's neck.

"What ever happened to doctor patient confidentiality?" Malachi snaps.

"There's a story there," I say. "And one I definitely want to hear. But not right now."

Nate chuckles and gathers the last of the supplies scattered on the floor. "It's a good story too."

"Thanks for coming, doc," Malachi says. "Don't you need to get back to the casino?"

"Yeah, yeah. I'm going." Nate makes his way down the stairs, but calls out, "I'll be back tomorrow to check on Peppermint."

When we're alone, I rock back on my feet. "So, now what?"

Before Malachi can answer, the door to Peppermint's room opens and Harlow steps out. I try to step around her before she can shut it, but she blocks my path.

"First, we talk," Harlow says. I glare at her, but she stands her ground. "Downstairs, both of you."

She moves between Malachi and me to go down the steps, not bothering to check if we're following. And because neither of us has a death wish, we do indeed follow.

Harlow heads straight for the bar, and Malachi double checks that the clubhouse door is locked. Satisfied that it is, he joins us at the bar and slides on the stool next to mine.

"Here." Harlow slides a beer to each of us and then lifts her own to her lips to take a long pull from the bottle. "This is a clusterfuck, you know that, right?" Her question is directed at me.

"I'm aware."

She shifts her gaze to Malachi, and her eyes soften. "I'm only going to ask this once. Did you know?"

He shakes his head. "No."

Harlow nods and then returns her attention to me. "There's a lot I didn't know until a few minutes ago." I open my mouth to speak, and she holds her hand up to stop me. "Let me finish." When she's convinced I'll be quiet, she continues. "Based on your reaction to her attack, I'm guessing you didn't know who Peppermint was until earlier. Please tell me I'm not wrong."

"You're not," I assure her. "Harlow, I promise you, I would never hurt her. I had no clue she was the girl from way back then."

Harlow presses her lips together and averts her gaze. When she looks back at me, there are tears in her eyes. Malachi sees them and rushes behind the bar to wrap his arms around her. She leans into him, taking the comfort he's offering, and I swear, she immediately looks stronger for it.

"Is she okay?" I ask, unable to pretend Peppermint isn't upstairs and hurt because of something I was a part of.

"She will be." Harlow's tone holds a hint of conviction. She might not believe what she's saying but she'll do everything in her power to make it true.

"What did she tell you?"

Harlow laughs, but there is no humor in it. "A lot, actually. But if you really want to know, you'll have to ask her. It's her story to tell, not mine."

"I'm going to assume that's why you never told me that Peppermint was a victim of our family," Malachi says.

"And you're assuming right," she confirms. "All of my sisters have stories, just like me. Just like the two of you. If and when they want someone to know, they'll tell them."

"Understood."

"That being said, Nico, there are several things I want you to know."

"Okay."

"First, you need to know that Pep knows you didn't rape her." A rush of air expels past my lips and Harlow's expression softens. "Second, you should know what triggered her. You whispered in her ear tonight, and that's when—"

"She remembered that I whispered in her ear all those years ago," I finish for her. "Yanni was forcing me to inject her, and just before I did, I whispered 'I'm sorry'."

"Motherfucker," Malachi mutters.

"Yes," Harlow confirms. "I asked her why she thought that you whispering in her ear was the specific trigger. I mean, we've been hunting Nicholi for so long, she's seen pictures, and she's talked to you enough times. But she never recognized either of you."

"And?"

Harlow shrugs. "She didn't have an answer."

"The mind is funny that way," I say. "It was probably her subconscious protecting her from the memories."

"Right."

The three of us are silent for a few minutes as we finish our beers. Malachi throws the empty bottles in the trash, and the clinking of the glass seems to echo in the large space.

Harlow clears her throat. "I need a favor, Nico."

Her tone suggests she's about to ask me to do something I won't like and that makes me uneasy.

"What?"

She takes a deep breath. "Fuck, I'm gonna regret this."

"Just spit it out."

"I know Peppermint is going to do her best to avoid you. Even if you were forced to do what you did, you were there for the worst part of her life."

"Okay." I drag the word out.

"Don't let her."

"Are you sure about this, *bella?*" my cousin prods.

"No," she admits to him. "But she can't keep hiding from her memories. Nico was just a kid, a victim like the others." Harlow smiles at me. "And you're family. You belong here, which means that she will never be able to avoid you completely."

"Nicholi is family too," I remind her, even if the words taste like acid on my tongue.

"No," she snaps. "He's not. He shares DNA, but DNA doesn't make you family. Blood doesn't equate to a get out of jail free card."

"She's not going to like this."

"Oh, I'm aware. Pep is going to fight this with everything in her." Harlow grins. "But she's not gonna stand a chance."

"What makes you think that?" I ask.

"Because you are persistent as hell. No matter what she throws at you, what body part she threatens to chop off, you don't stop. You keep coming back for more. There are only two things that make a man as relentless as you've been. The first is a death wish, and I'm pretty sure you're not looking for a way out of this crazy train of life."

"Definitely not a death wish," I confirm. "What's the second?"

"Love, Nico. The only other reason a man is as tenacious as you are with a woman is love. You, my soon to be cousin-in-law, are in love with my best friend. And I, for one, am here for it because Peppermint deserves the kind of love a good Ricci man can give her."

CHAPTER 7

Peppermint

"IT FUCKIN' stinks in here."

I roll toward the wall and pull the blanket over my head. Spooks isn't the most empathetic person, so Harlow must really be at her wits end with me if she's sending our Sergeant at Arms in to do her dirty work.

"Go away."

The blanket is ripped from my body, and I'm dragged by the waistband of my sweats to the edge of the mattress.

"Not happening," Spooks quips. Her tone is light as if she's enjoying this. Shit, she probably is. "You've been in your room for a week, and judging by the stench, you haven't showered."

"No one else seemed to care."

There's been a parade of people through my door. Everyone has made an appearance, even some of the escorts.

"Bitch, they cared. They were just too polite to say anything." Spooks grabs my arm and pulls until I'm forced to stand up. "Shower, now."

I yank out of her grip, my anger struggling against its tether, begging to be unleashed. "Remember who you're talking to," I command.

"When you start acting like you outrank me, I'll remember that you do."

Muscle memory kicks in, and I bend to grab my knife, but my hand comes away empty.

Spooks laughs.

"Aw, don't you hate it when that happens?"

Out of the corner of my eye, I catch sight of my sheath on my nightstand, but before I can make a move for it, Spooks wraps her hand around my wrist. She hauls me into the bathroom and turns on the shower.

"You can get in on your own, or I'll throw you in." I grimace but don't budge. "Throw you in it is then."

She wraps her arms around my body like she's going to pick me up, and I give in.

"Fine," I shout, shoving her away from me. "I'll get a fucking shower." Spooks straightens and crosses her arms over her chest. "I said I'll get in."

"I heard you. But I think I'll just stay right here to make sure."

"Cunt," I mumble as I strip my clothes off.

"I've been called worse."

Stepping over the edge of the tub, I can't stop the moan that escapes as the warm water cascades down my body. Spooks snickers, but wisely keeps her mouth shut. After a few minutes, I hear Spooks leave the bathroom, but I don't hear the sound of my bedroom door open, which tells me I'm still going to have to deal with her when I'm done.

I stay in the shower far longer than it takes to get clean, only getting out when the water turns cold. With a towel wrapped around my chest, I glance in the mirror. My face is a swirl of yellow and green and the stitched cut is slowly healing. Nate told me when he stopped by yesterday that the stitches could probably come out in a few days.

Grabbing a second towel, I wrap it around my hair and stalk into the bedroom. Spooks is sitting on my bed, which now has fresh sheets, and there's a small stack of clothes folded next to her. My cut is on the top.

"Get dressed and meet me in the hall," she says. She stands to leave me alone to do her bidding, but doubles back and snags my knife off the nightstand. "You can have this once you're done."

Once I'm alone, I finish drying off and get dressed. I'll never admit it, but it feels good to do something normal. This past week has been… difficult. I know holing up in my room was stupid, but I couldn't work up the motivation to do anything else. Harlow made sure I ate, and she only accomplished that because the gnawing feeling in my stomach was getting on my nerves.

I slip my cut on and open the door to find Spooks leaning against the wall. "Now what?" I ask.

"Now the fun begins." She hands me my sheath, but there's no knife in it. When I narrow my eyes on her, she shrugs. "You'll get it soon, I promise." She pushes off the wall and starts down the steps. "C'mon, P. Time's wastin'."

I roll my eyes but follow her down the stairs. The main room of the clubhouse is busy, especially for a weekday.

Is it a weekday?

Shit, I don't even know.

"Ignore everyone and keep walking," Spooks instructs without looking back at me.

We head outside, and she leads me to my favorite place: the targets. The leaves rustle in the trees, and I instantly feel a sense of calm wash over me. Spooks stops on the throwing line and turns to hand me my knife.

"How'd you know?" I ask, taking the knife from her.

"What? That this is what you needed?"

"Yeah."

"What sane, rational woman doesn't need to throw sharp objects at targets every once in a while?" she counters.

"Do you feel better?"

I hop up on the stool next to Harlow and grin. "Much," I admit.

I don't know how long I stayed at the targets, but my throwing arm is sore, and the sun is starting to dip below the horizon.

"Can I get a water, Fiona?" I ask our bartender.

"Make that two," Harlow adds. "And see if there's any more pizza left in the kitchen for P."

"You got it." Fiona sets two bottles of water in front of us before going into the kitchen. She comes back with a full plate. "There were only four slices, but I can send one of the girls to get more if you want."

"Four slices is plenty, thanks."

It takes all of five minutes to polish off three slices, and when I lean back and rub my stomach, Harlow snags the last piece and practically inhales it.

"Where's Malachi?" I ask, spinning around to look out over the main room.

"He's at Nico's place getting the last of his security system set up."

My heart rate speeds up at the mention of the man who sent me spiraling. I don't know what I expected but hearing that he's going to be in Atlantic City long enough to have a place and need a security system installed isn't it.

"He's been asking about you, ya know? Shows up here every day and sits outside your bedroom door in case you open it."

"Who?" I ask, although I already know.

Not only has he continued to send me my daily morning texts, but Nico also talks to me from the other side of the door. I don't respond, but I know he's there. And despite my reaction to him a week ago, a sense of peace washes over me when I hear him. I can't explain it, so I don't even bother bringing it up.

"Seriously, Pep? You know damn well who."

"What have you told him?"

"Nothing beyond that you're healing."

"Am I, Har? Healing?" I hug my waist and think about how fucked up I am to be terrified of a man who also makes things better. "I mean, I know I'm physically improving. And yeah, I guess I am mentally, too, but…"

"But what?"

"What if I'm triggered again?" That's the biggest question that stops me from opening that damn door.

"Then we deal with it," she responds, as if losing my shit is nothing to worry about. Harlow sighs and bumps my shoulder with hers. "But I think you're more scared that you might not get triggered, that Nico will crash through all the walls and defenses you've carefully crafted over the years."

"I let people in."

"You let *me* in. *Me*, Pep. I'm one person. Besides you kept a lot of barriers in place until last week, so I'm not sure I even count."

"Bullshit. I've let all our sisters in. And I let Malachi in, didn't I?"

"You can argue with me all you want, but deep down, you know I'm right. The people who were supposed to love you unconditionally, didn't, and because of that, you don't invite anyone close enough to risk that kind of pain again. I get it, P. I really do. You know that about me better than anyone." Harlow rests a hand on my shoulder. "But maybe it's time to open yourself up a little. Take a risk. You've got the support and the love of not only me, but also of all the DHMC sisters and Malachi. Jump, P. I promise you we'll be there to catch you if you fall."

She leans in and kisses me on the cheek before hopping off her stool and walking to join the others at the pool table.

Now what the fuck am I supposed to do?

CHAPTER 8
Nico

SUN STREAMS THROUGH THE WINDOW, and I curse myself for not remembering to pull the blinds down before climbing into bed last night. I roll away from the offending light, tugging the black Egyptian cotton sheet over my face. As sleep begins to drag me back under, my cell phone chimes with a notification.

"You've got to be kidding me," I mumble.

Without moving my head from under the sheet, I blindly reach my hand out and pat around my nightstand until my fingers hit the phone. I bring the cell close to my face and squint, trying to make out the text. It takes a second, but it quickly comes into focus and what I read sends my pulse skittering.

Peppermint: Morning.

One thousand percent sure I'm reading it wrong, I rub my eyes with a fist to clear the sleep from them. I read the text again, and then a third time before it sinks in that my tired brain isn't deceiving me.

I push the sheet away and slide up the bed to lean against

the wall, groaning at the cold surface. I have a headboard ordered, but the company will only deliver it when I'm home and that hasn't been much this past week. All of my belongings were shipped from Seattle, but the fucking bed frame was damaged in transit.

I type out a response to Peppermint but delete it and start again. I don't get the text sent before another message pops up from her.

Peppermint: Are you seriously going to ignore me?

Chuckling at her impatience, I delete my text again and peck out another one.

Me: Morning sunshine.

Peppermint: Sunshine? Have you even met me?

Me: You're right, I have.

I hit send but immediately begin typing again.

Me: Morning my little ray of pitch black.

Me: There, is that better?

Peppermint: Little bit, yeah.

Me: How are you feeling today?

Peppermint: I'll be there in ten minutes. There better be coffee.

Me: What? You're coming here?

I stare at the screen waiting for a response. A full minute passes with nothing.

Me: Hello? Answer me.

Still nothing.

Me: Did I understand you right? You're coming to my place?

When I don't get a response after another two minutes—I fucking counted—I toss my phone onto the mattress and race to the bathroom. I've never been so grateful that I sleep naked because I'd surely fall and break something if I had to strip while I'm rushing.

I take the quickest shower of my life, and as I brush my teeth, the distinct rumble of a motorcycle snags my attention.

Shit.

After spitting the toothpaste into the sink, I rinse the bowl and dry my mouth on the towel. I snag a pair of black sweats from my dresser but don't bother with anything else as I listen for her to knock on the door.

I grab my cell phone to check the time. It's been exactly ten minutes since her last text. I don't know if I'm more impressed with her ability to be right on time or the speed with which I got ready.

By the time I reach the living room, I still haven't heard her knock, so I open the door thinking she's just taking her sweet time. There's no one on the porch. I lean around the door frame to peer at the driveway. Her Harley is backed up to the garage door, but Peppermint is nowhere to be seen.

"You're not very observant."

I whirl around and see Peppermint standing next to my leather sectional, her head tilted to the side like she's trying to figure me out.

"What are…" I glance at the door and then back to her. "How'd you…" I shut the door and flip the deadbolt before facing her fully. "Did you break into my house?"

"I don't know what you paid for your security system, but it's garbage."

I turn to look at the keypad by the door, tapping the screen several times to determine why the alarm didn't sound the minute she opened the door. When I realize what happened, I hang my head.

"You forgot to set it, didn't you?" she asks as she steps up next to me.

I take a deep breath and nod. "Apparently."

It's quiet for a moment, the only sound in the room our combined breathing. Heat radiates off her, and I have to make a conscious effort not to lean into the warmth.

"Can you go put a shirt on?" she asks softly and turns to face me. "This…" Peppermint waves her hand up and down to indicate my torso. "It's distracting."

I can't stop my lips from lifting into a smirk. "Nah, I'm good."

Peppermint moves away from me, toward the couch, but doesn't sit down. "I don't smell coffee."

"I haven't had a chance to make any."

I walk to the kitchen and ignore the fact that she sidesteps when I pass her. What I can't ignore is the way she watches my every move. Her stare is like a physical touch scorching my skin. As much as I tell myself that it's just her being wary, my dick doesn't get the memo and stands at attention.

"Not to look a gift horse in the mouth, but why are you here?"

Peppermint takes the mug I hold out to her and moves to sit at the island that separates the kitchen and living spaces. She blows on her coffee to cool it down, and my cock jerks at how her lips are pursed.

Fuck, those lips would feel good wrapped aro—

"I'm, uh…" She takes several deep breaths and a sip of coffee. "I'm sorry about that," she says, nodding at my chest.

I shrug as if getting sliced open by the love of your life is no big deal. "I've had worse."

"Yeah, I saw."

I narrow my eyes, wondering what she's talking about, and it dawns on me. When I was at the door, she was behind me. She saw the whip scars.

"Angelo Ricci was a hard man."

"Your father was a sadistic bastard who needed to inflict pain in order to feel powerful, in order to assert his dominance."

The way she averts her eyes tells me more than she probably realizes. Yanni and Nicholi—and me if I'm being honest —aren't the only ones who hurt her all those years ago.

"You speak from experience."

I'm stating the obvious, but she needs to know that I hear what she's not saying. I see what she's trying like hell not to show me. Trauma recognizes trauma.

Rather than risk giving anything more away, Peppermint quietly sips her coffee. The silence stretches, and when it becomes deafening, I have no other choice but to break it.

"I'm sorry I triggered you." The words are inadequate, but they're all I have.

Peppermint's expression hardens. She's anchoring her defenses, barricading herself behind brick walls. I let her, knowing that I'll keep chipping away, brick by brick, until there's nothing left to stop me from making her mine.

"What's going on in that head of yours?" I ask, genuinely curious.

Peppermint slides her mug across the counter and rises from the stool. I watch as she paces, back and forth, back and forth, her boots thudding on the hardwood. She opens and closes her mouth several times as if she's going to answer, but nothing comes out.

"Why me?" she finally cries, stopping in front of me.

There are so many things she can be referring to, so I blurt out the first thing that comes to mind.

"Because you are everything that is perfect in this world." I reach out to touch her cheek, but she backs away. Shoving my hands in my pockets, I sigh. "Your strength is unparalleled. You're smart, funny, determined, and you're beautiful. So fucking beautiful."

"You forgot stubborn, short-tempered, and carrying around a shit load of baggage and rage." She snaps her fingers. "Oh, and great with a blade." I laugh at that but quickly sober when she glares at me. "But that's not what I meant."

"I'm not following."

"Why me?" she repeats, throwing her hands up. "Why was I taken? What was it that made me a target for your family?"

My heart stutters at the utter heartbreak in her tone. Instinct has me moving forward, but fear pulls her away.

"You existed," I say simply. "You were born into a world where evil lurks around every corner. Your only flaw is that you don't have any flaws." She snorts at that. "You exist, *cuore mio,* and for my family, that was enough."

She stares at me like she's searching for some hidden meaning in my words, but she won't find any. My family, and those who supported them, was atrocious. I come from a toxic bloodline.

"I hate when you call me that," she mutters.

"I know."

"Then why do you keep doing it?"

"Because one of these days, you're not going to hate it."

CHAPTER 9
Peppermint

"LOOK AT ME."

I shake my head against the onslaught of emotions that have been battering me since the moment I stepped inside his house. Ignoring Nico's command, I distance myself from him and flop down on the sectional. I can't look at him because I have no clue what version of him will be looking back.

Will it be the brutal version, the one where all I see is Nicholi? Or will it be the best version, the one who is all Nico, the man who, although I won't admit it out loud, puts a smile on my face without even trying?

"I'm not him."

"I know."

"Do you?" Nico counters. He crouches in front of me and grips my chin to force me to look at him. "I can't help the fact that I'm a replica of your nightmares, but I promise you that what is on the inside…" He taps his chest. "What's in here is the exact opposite of that."

When I remain quiet, he drops his hand and falls back to sit on the floor. "What do you want from me, Pep? Why did you come here this morning?"

I came to face my fear.

"I don't—"

My cell rings and I'm grateful for the distraction. I pull it out of my cut and, seeing that it's Harlow, I press the phone icon.

"Hey, Prez, what's up?"

"You need to get to Umbria's Universe," she says, referring to the casino that Malachi runs.

"What's going on?" I ask.

Nico's cell pings and he takes it from his pocket, frowning when he looks at the screen. He's up on his feet and disappearing down the hall in seconds.

"Just get here, P," Harlow snaps.

I make my way toward the door. "I'm on my way."

I disconnect the call and shove the device back into my cut. I turn to yell out that I'm leaving and collide with Nico's hard chest. Lowering my eyes, I see that he's fully dressed.

"I gotta go," we blurt out simultaneously.

"Umbria's?" he asks.

"Yep."

Nico locks the door behind us, and I want to ask him if he set the alarm but decide to keep my mouth shut. He's a big boy and if he forgets again, that's on him.

"Uh, what're you doing?" I ask when he straddles my Harley behind me.

"I'm riding with you," he says as if him being on the back of my motorcycle is a completely normal thing.

"You're lucky I don't have time to argue," I grumble and fire up the bike. "If you fall off, I'm not stopping," I shout.

Nico's chest rumbles against my back when he laughs. I tear out of the driveway and through the residential neighborhood, going as fast as I can. The normally twenty-minute ride is reduced to fifteen. I go around back to the employee parking lot and am surprised to see Harlow and Malachi outside talking to Coast, Fiona's old man.

"This can't be good," Nico comments after I cut the engine.

"What the hell is going on?" I call out as we walk across the lot.

"See for yourself," Harlow responds. She swipes her key card and opens the door so we can all step inside. "One of the Blackjack dealers found her when he came this way to head out for a smoke break."

I stare at the dead woman on the floor. Her bright red lipstick is smeared, and her left eye is swollen shut. The black dress she was wearing is torn and bunched around her waist. If she was wearing panties or a bra, they're missing.

"She one of yours?" I ask Malachi.

"No," he responds.

"She's one of ours," Harlow adds. "Her name's Tasha. I hired her on a trial basis last week while you were…" She sighs. "She started last week."

"Was she a victim?" I ask, knowing that we permit our adult female victims to become escorts, if that's the path they want to take. Surprisingly, some do because it's all they know. We make it worthwhile for them and they become part of the family, so to speak.

Harlow shakes her head. "She came in looking for a job, but Devil's isn't hiring so I offered her this instead. She had a little boy with her, and it was pretty obvious she needed the money. After calling her sister to make sure she was willing to babysit while she worked, she accepted the job."

"If she's tied to DHMC, what's she doing here?" Nico asks.

"That's the million-dollar question," Coast pipes in.

I turn to face the cop. "And you're here because…"

"I called him," Malachi responds before Coast can. "The employee who found her kept insisting that the cops be called. Rather than risk him calling 911, I called Coast."

"I took his statement, talked to him for a minute," Coast

says and shrugs. "Basically made him feel like he was heard and that this wouldn't get swept under the rug. That seemed to satisfy him."

"Does this fucker still have a job?" I ask, annoyed that Malachi gave in to some idiot who probably watches too many reruns of Law and Order.

Malachi smirks. "Gill escorted him off the property right before you got here."

"Good."

"I gotta run," Coast says. "If you decide to call this in, let me know so I can request to be assigned to the case. Otherwise, I know nothing."

"Thanks, man." Harlow slaps him on the back. "Appreciate you coming so quickly."

"Don't thank me." He chuckles. "Fiona's the one who got shortchanged this morning when your call came in."

Coast leaves us with the body. Nico crouches down next to her, and his eyes scan her beaten and bloody frame. He lifts her right arm, then her left, then straightens to his full height.

"You know this is Nicholi, right?" Nico says. "It's the only thing that makes sense. Who else would kill a DHMC escort and leave her on a Ricci doorstep, so to speak?"

"That's our thought too," Harlow agrees.

"This has to stop," I snap. "We know he's here, in Atlantic City, and we know he's trying to get back in the skin trade. How the fuck do we stop him? Because I'm getting damn tired of him being five steps ahead of us."

"We're bringing this to Church. Pep, send a text letting everyone know to meet at the clubhouse in an hour. We're not sitting on this one. It's time to end this."

"You're not cutting us out of this," Nico snarls.

Harlow steps up to Nico and stabs a finger at his chest. "Our escort, our problem."

Nico puffs his chest out. Before he can get a word out, Malachi yanks him away from Harlow.

"Don't," he growls. "Square up to my woman like that again and I'm liable to forget I actually love your stupid ass."

Nico lifts his hands and takes one step back. "Got it." Malachi gives a curt nod. "But I'll be damned if I'm going to sit by and let them handle this."

"It's not your call," I snap.

Nico rounds on me. Part of me expects Malachi or Harlow to stop him, but they don't.

"He's my brother. I didn't get to take out the rest of the trash, and I won't let you take this from me too."

"Mal, handle him," Harlow orders.

Malachi narrows his eyes. "No, *bella*."

"Excuse me?"

"You heard me. I'm with Nico on this. You're not cutting us out."

"Are you forgetting who I am?"

"I know exactly who you are," Malachi counters. "If anyone is forgetting anything, it's you. We agreed that I won't interfere with club business, and you won't interfere with family business." Harlow opens her mouth to protest but Malachi covers it with his palm. "This, *madam president*, concerns us all. So we will work together on it, like we have been for the past year."

I quickly turn away to hide my grin. I love Harlow like a sister, and I will have her back no matter what. But it's comical as hell to watch a man she once loathed try to put her in her place.

"Fine," Harlow capitulates stiffly. "We'll work together."

Oh shit. Malachi is definitely going to pay for this later.

"Wise choice," Nico grits.

Harlow glares at Nico, and if looks could kill, he'd be dead. As it stands, he's practically a dead man walking because I'm not exactly thrilled with his attitude either.

Men should not fuck with women who play with sharp objects like a toddler plays with Play-Doh.

CHAPTER 10
Nico

"THAT'S SOME BULLSHIT."

I laugh at Gill, head of security for the casino and one of our best employees at Forza Security. The indignation on his face is so comical that I can't resist egging him on.

"I guess she likes me better than you."

Gill stops walking and draws his gun on me. "Take that back," he demands.

"Put that away," Malachi orders. "He's fucking with you, man."

Gill glares at me for a beat longer, then holsters his weapon. "I can't believe she didn't threaten you with the hatchet," he grumbles. "I'm gonna have to talk to her. She's going soft."

He starts walking again, leaving Malachi and me to follow.

"You couldn't leave well enough alone, could you?" Malachi deadpans.

"He makes it so easy. Besides, who would've expected the big guy to get all butt hurt that we still have our balls?"

"You know as well as I do how hard he's worked to get on

Harlow's good side. He's sensitive about the whole hatchet thing."

"I'm not sensitive," Gill barks over his shoulder.

"Whatever you say, man," I tease.

Gill reaches the meeting room at the clubhouse and when he steps inside, I grab Malachi's arm to stop him.

"What?"

"Dude's got a point. Why do we still have our balls?"

Malachi throws his head back and laughs. When he sobers, he rests a hand on my shoulder. "Oh, I'm going to pay for my words later. Harlow will make sure of it. But I like the hatchet as much as she does, and she knows it. You, on the other hand... Peppermint's going to fuck your world up."

"Great. Like she needs a damn blade to do that."

"Be afraid, cuz. Be very afraid."

Malachi practically skips the rest of the way down the hall. Okay, so he doesn't skip at all, but it's what I imagine the pussy-whipped asshole does. The image makes me feel a little better.

I step over the threshold into the room and am immediately shoved against the wall. Harlow's standing in front of me with her hatchet pressed against my throat and an arm across my chest. Peppermint is next to her, her serrated knife tip way too close to my groin.

"Do not mistake my acquiescence for weakness," Harlow snarls.

"Never said you were weak," I tell her and lower my eyes to Peppermint. "Uh, can you move that thing? It's a little too close for comfort."

Peppermint presses the tip against the zipper of my jeans. "Nah, I like it right where it is."

"What's it gonna take for you both to back off?"

"I don't know," Harlow says and turns her head to look at Peppermint. "What do you think, Pep?"

"Hmm." Peppermint tilts her head and pretends to think it over. "Silence."

"I like that," Harlow says.

"Silence?"

"Yeah," Peppermint confirms. "As in sit down and keep your mouth shut."

"What about Malachi?" I ask.

Harlow looks over her shoulder at her other half. "He knows what's expected of him inside this room."

"You tell 'em," Gill prods from his position at the end of the table.

"Any more questions?" Harlow asks me.

"Nope."

"Good." She lowers her hatchet, and Peppermint backs up as well. Harlow whirls around and faces Gill. "Next time you want to make a point, do it yourself."

"While this has been entertaining as hell, can we get down to business?" Giggles asks before dropping into her chair. "I've gotta pick Noah up from school in an hour."

"You heard her," Harlow says and moves to the head of the table. "Let's get started."

For the next thirty minutes, I sit quietly and listen to all the women discuss my twin and brainstorm ways to locate and eliminate him. At one point, I stand, but Malachi yanks me back down and elbows me in the gut so I can't say anything.

"I hate to throw a wrench in things," Spooks, the scariest of all the DHMC members, begins. "But what makes you think we'll be able to find Nicholi? He's evaded us for a year. I'm not real clear how anything has changed."

"I'm here," I say quietly, which earns me a glare from Peppermint and another elbow in the gut from Malachi.

"Nico, dude, you suck at following directions." Harlow shakes her head. "That being said, you're right." She scans the faces of her sisters. "I don't think Nicholi will be able to stay hidden with Nico here. He's going to want to face his brother and that need for revenge is what will drive him out of hiding."

"Add me into the mix, and he definitely won't be able to resist."

I shoot up from my chair, unable to stay quiet at Peppermint's statement. "What the fuck is that supposed to mean?" I stalk toward where she's sitting. "You're not getting added to shit, so get that thought out of your head."

Peppermint rises and pushes her chair out of the way as she spins around to face me. "I'm a big girl, Nico. I can handle myself."

"Like you did last time you went up against him," I counter. "He knocked you on your ass then and he'll do that and worse if given a second chance."

Peppermint presses her lips together and her cheeks darken with fury. The moment the words were out of my mouth, I knew I fucked up, but it's too late now.

"What exactly do you think I've been doing for the last year? Sitting on my ass while everyone else runs into danger?"

"Of course not. But I'm here now so you don't have to."

"You were there years ago too!" she screams.

Without thinking, I thrust my arm out and wrap my hand around her throat. I'm dimly aware of the others in the room jumping to their feet and circling the wagons, but I can't see past the film of rage Peppermint's provoked in me.

"I couldn't do a goddamn thing back then," I growl. She claws at my hand, but I don't let go. Even in my current state, I'm aware enough to temper my strength so I know I'm not actually hurting her. "I can now. And if you think I'm going to sit idly by and eat fucking popcorn while he does his worst to you, think again."

"Let her go."

I shift my eyes to take in Harlow and am not at all

surprised to see her holding her hatchet. In fact, the entirety of the DHMC officers have some form of weapon drawn at me. Each has an identical murderous glint in their eyes and no doubt matching hate in their hearts.

"Nico," Malachi prods.

My brain is screaming at me to remove my hand from her neck, to back away slowly and grovel for forgiveness. But my brain checked out of the equation the second Peppermint screamed at me and threw my past deeds in my face. I'm running on primal emotion and all of it is dark.

"I'm fine," Peppermint assures them all without taking her eyes off me.

"I don't give a shit if you're fine or not," Spooks spits out. "No man puts his hands on you."

"Har, stand down," Peppermint says. "Please."

The two women exchange a look and something in Peppermint's eyes must reassure Harlow because she lowers the hatchet. The rest follow suit, but none of them move.

"Gill, you too," Harlow commands.

The big man lets loose a string of words that would make a sailor blush, but he holsters his gun.

"Nico," Peppermint begins. "I'm only going to say this once so listen carefully." She lets her body relax, which increases the pressure of my grip. I loosen my hold to accommodate. "I am not a sit-back-and-let-the-men-handle-the-hard-stuff kinda woman. You know this. You want to protect me, I get that. And if I'm being honest, I don't hate that you want to. It's actually kinda nice." I let out a low rumble, and she fucking grins. "But we're either in this together, fifty-fifty, or not at all."

I replay her words in my head, mulling them over while I try to come up with a response. The problem is, I keep getting caught up on the word 'together'. What the hell is she referring to? Taking down Nicholi, or more?

"Together or not at all," she repeats.

You'll never know what she means if you don't let her go and ride it out.

"Together," I echo.

I rub my thumb gently over her flesh and revel at the goosebumps my touch causes to erupt. Peppermint's pupils dilate and her lips part. And because I'm human, my body reacts. I lean forward and press my lips to her ear, praying like hell that I don't trigger her.

"I will always choose together, *cuore mio*," I whisper.

I brace myself for an attack, but it doesn't come.

Instead, my feisty spitfire shivers.

CHAPTER 11
Peppermint

"WHAT THE FUCK WAS THAT?"

I shrug. Only Harlow and I remain in the meeting room, as she dismissed the others after voting on a plan for Nicholi. Nico tried to stay, but Spooks dragged him out the door. I absently rub my neck, my skin still on fire where he touched.

"Bullshit," Harlow barks. "If I'm not mistaken, you liked his hands on you."

I lift my head and lock eyes with her. I could lie, but she'd know. She always knows. Lowering my arm to the table, I rest my head on my forearm.

"What am I gonna do, Har?"

"Straddle him like he's a limited-edition Harley and ride him into the sunset."

"I'm being serious." My words are muffled by my arm, but I don't bother moving.

"So am I."

I release a groan. "I don't even know what to say to you right now."

"How about, 'yes, Prez, I'll get right on it… er, I mean him… I'll get right on him'?" There's a teasing lilt to her words, but she's not joking. When I remain silent, she continues. "Okay, fine. You want my honest opinion?"

I lift my head. "Yes!"

"It's the same as it was yesterday. If you like him, go for it."

"It's a little more complicated than that."

"Is it?"

"He's my nightmare's twin. Of course, it is."

"Pep, the man wrapped his hand around your throat, and I swear you smiled."

"I didn't smile," I argue. And I didn't. Not on the outside anyway.

"Your panty hamster sure did. That bitch lit up like a firework finale."

"Fuck you," I mutter.

"You're missing the point entirely. I'm already getting fucked. Nico is who I'm suggesting you—"

"Ya know, regular sex has turned you into a hussy," I accuse as I get up. "It's annoying."

"Yet you're still here, with me, hoping I say whatever it is that you want to hear."

"Isn't that what best friends are for?"

"Nope. Best friends are there to tell you like it is without sugarcoating anything."

"Well, you've got that shit down to an art form."

"Thank you."

"It wasn't a compliment," I mumble as I walk to the door.

Harlow falls into step beside me when I'm halfway down the hall and throws her arm around my shoulder. I try to turn toward the stairs when we reach the main room, but she steers me toward the bar instead.

"I need to grab something out of my room."

"No, you don't. You're trying to flee and hide. I'm not stupid."

"Never said you were."

"Ladies," Malachi greets when we reach the end of the bar where he and Nico are sitting.

I do my best not to look at Nico but fail miserably. Butter-flies start salsa dancing in my stomach at the heat in his stare. And based on the wink he just gave me, he knows exactly the effect he's having on me.

"You okay, Pep?" Malachi asks me, his brow arched.

"Yeah," I croak. After clearing my throat, I repeat myself. "Yeah, I'm good."

"Are you sure because you look a little flushed." He flattens his hand on my forehead. "Nope, no fever."

"I'm fine," I say from behind clenched teeth and smack his hand away.

"If you say so." He turns to Harlow and wraps his arms around her. "Whaddya say we get outta here? We should pop back in at both casinos, but then we can head home."

Harlow glances at me as if making sure I'm okay to be left alone with Nico. I roll my eyes at her, and she takes that as a yes.

"So ready," she purrs. She grabs his hand and practically drags him to the door. "Don't do anything I wouldn't do," she calls over her shoulder.

"It's going to be hard to work together if you keep trying to avoid me."

I slowly turn around, a sharp retort on the tip of my tongue, but nothing comes out when my gaze lands on Nico. He really is a sexy man. And the fact that I think so is more than a little disturbing... considering.

"You're staring."

Yes, yes I am.

Nico slides off his stool and closes the distance between us. Without touching me, he urges me to turn and back up against the edge of the bar. He leans forward and braces his hands on either side of me to cage me in.

He's close. So fucking close. And I'm wet. My eyes slide closed. So fucking wet.

What the hell?

"I'd love to take care of that for you," he croons, and my eyes fly open. "Yeah, you said it out loud."

Nico's chocolate brown eyes are hooded, and his arms are inching closer to my body. Embers of lust skitter from one nerve ending to the next until my entire being feels as if I'm on fire.

When Nico lifts a hand and tucks his finger under my chin, I swear I hear a sizzle. "This is gonna happen. Sooner rather than later, I'm sure." He leans forward and lightly presses his lips to mine for the briefest of seconds. "But not here. And not yet."

A groan escapes me, and he chuckles. "I need to know that you are crystal fucking clear about whose cock is inside you when we fuck. And you're not quite there, are you?"

Am I? I want Nico, there's no denying that. But that's the only thing I'm sure of. And knowing how he feels about me only complicates things. Because even if I could get past who he resembles, that doesn't mean there are feelings attached.

No, I'm not that cold-hearted.

Nico heaves a sigh and backs away from me. "That's what I thought."

"Nico, I'm—"

"Please don't apologize, Peppermint. I can handle a lot of things, but you saying you're sorry for doing what's best for you isn't one of them. You apologizing for having trauma that *my* family caused isn't one of them."

And just like that, several bricks fall from the walls around my heart.

CHAPTER 12

Nico

AFTER PARKING my car in the garage, I walk around to the front porch, my gun drawn. I carry the 9mm at all times, and right this minute, I'm glad I do. I tiptoe up the steps and stare at the broken glass and ajar front door. Whoever the fuck broke into my house is about to meet his, or her, maker.

Before entering, I pull out my cell and shoot off a quick text to Malachi.

Me: House broken into. Going in.

I turn the ringer off in case he responds. No need to give an intruder the heads up that they've been caught. And even if Malachi responds, he'll still come running. Or he'll send Gill. I'm okay with either of them, as long as I get back-up.

I quietly push the door the rest of the way open and wince when it creaks on its hinges. I make a mental note to WD-40 the fucking thing and keep moving. It takes all of two seconds to realize that whoever broke in, they were searching for something. My sectional is sliced to shreds, the stuffing littering the floor like an exploded teddy bear.

If I hadn't just left the clubhouse, I'd think the DHMC was

responsible. They don't hide the fact that they inflict damage with sharp weapons and this reeks of their MO. But no, it's not them. I'm family now.

After quickly clearing the kitchen, laundry room, and half bath on the first floor, I climb the stairs. The more of the house I see, the more infuriated I become. Not only is everything torn apart, but there are numerous holes in the walls, along with what I hope is paint splattered everywhere.

The spare room and my office are clear, albeit messy as fuck. My bedroom is the only room remaining, and when I step inside, bile crawls up my throat.

In the middle of my bed is a woman, or what was a woman. I force myself to turn away and check the attached bath. When I'm satisfied that no one remains in the house, no one *alive*, I retrace my steps and go closer to the bed. I take my cell back out of my pocket and send another text to Malachi.

Me: All clear. Need a body bag.

As I slide my phone back into my pocket, my eyes snag on the wall opposite me, and I freeze. The message written in blood tells me exactly who is responsible for all of this destruction.

Her blood is on your hands, Craig.
Who will be next, brother?

"Motherfucker."

"Who the hell is Craig?"

I whirl around and aim my 9mm, but swiftly lower it when I see Peppermint standing in the doorway.

"What are you doing here?"

"Malachi called me. I was closer than he was."

"Remind me to kill him later."

"Why, because he sent a girl to save you?"

"No. I'm going to kill him because he sent *you* into a potentially dangerous situation," I snarl.

"I bet she wishes someone was looking out for her like that." Peppermint tips her head to the woman on the mattress. "Who is Craig?"

"I'm Craig," I answer absently.

"Care to elaborate?"

"Craig Moore was the new identity my father saddled me with when he shipped me off to Seattle."

"Huh. When did you take your real name back?"

"Is this a conversation that can wait? I think we've got more important things to deal with."

"Right." Peppermint walks to the bed and takes in the eviscerated woman. "Do you know her?"

I step up beside her and look at the pristine face of my former personal assistant. It was ingrained into anyone who worked for the Ricci Crime Family that the face was not to be touched. It should be left in pristine condition, so buyers felt like they were getting their money's worth.

"Yeah." I run a hand through my hair. "Her name is Bethany. She worked for me in Seattle."

"What the hell does he have against her?"

"Nothing," I snap. "Like you, her only crime is existing."

"I'm not buying it. He did this for a reason."

"He did it because he could. It's as simple and as fucked up as that."

"No." Peppermint shakes her head. "This wasn't the quick act of a man who kills just because he can. This took planning, it took work. He had to either lure her here under some false pretense or he traveled across the country and somehow convinced her to come back to New Jersey with him."

Fuck. She's right. But that means…

"He's been watching me." I turn away from Peppermint and slam my fist into the wall. "For years, he knew where I was, who I was. Fucking years!"

"Probably."

"How the hell are you so calm?" I thunder.

"Blood and death don't bother me," she says matter-of-factly. "And really, this isn't all that surprising."

"It sure as shit is to me."

"It shouldn't be. Nothing Nicholi does should surprise you. He was raised by your father, after all. The only reason you're not exactly like him is because you got to be someone else. You got away."

"I was sent away," I remind her. "Banished and treated like a pariah."

"Not by the people who mattered."

"Person. It was one person."

"You're right, it was only one person. But even you have to admit, having a person like Malachi in your corner kinda balances the scales a little."

"How do you figure?"

Peppermint grabs my hand and drags me out of the bedroom and downstairs. I should dig my heels in, stop her from treating me like a rag doll, but I can't. Not when she's voluntarily touching me.

Down, boy.

She guides me to the kitchen where she pushes me toward the only stool that's still in one piece. "Sorry. It was hard to have a conversation up there."

"Okay."

"Sit, Nico."

I do.

Why am I letting her order me around?

"Malachi balances the scales because he's good. He shouldn't be, not with how he was raised, just like your brother. But he is. And not only is he good, he's also a man who has turned the Ricci name from a dark stain on this city to a bright light in the remaining dark."

"Aw, listen to you waxing all poetic."

I straighten to look over Peppermint's shoulder and she turns around. Malachi whistles as he takes in the chaos that is my home.

"I'll deny ever having said a word of that," Peppermint barks.

"Don't worry, the fact that you're secretly in love with me will not make the rounds of the gossip mill," my cousin teases her.

Jealousy burns through me. "Back off, Mal," I snarl.

"Fucking hell," he mutters. "You're usually the one who can handle jokes."

"Not where Peppermint's concerned."

"Fine."

"What are you doing here, anyway?" Peppermint asks him, her hands on her hips. "I told you I'd handle it."

"I know." Malachi nods in my direction. "But he texted that there was a body, so I brought reinforcements."

Just as he finishes speaking, Harlow, Spooks, Gill, and Mama walk through my front door as if they own the place.

"Come on in," I grumble.

"Thanks, we will." Spooks grins. "Where's the body?"

I point toward the stairs. "Last door on the right."

Spooks and Mama head up the steps, while Harlow, Gill, and Malachi traipse through the remnants of my sectional to stand closer to Peppermint and me.

"I'll have another house secured for you by nightfall," Malachi says.

"Thanks, I appreciate it."

"You could always stay at the clubhouse," Harlow offers.

"No."

Peppermint and I speak at the same time.

"In that case, Peppermint, you'll be staying with Nico at his new place," Harlow states. "And before you can argue, this isn't a request. It's an order."

"Gill, you'll be stationed outside the home, along with

several others, to keep watch," Malachi adds. "You can pick your team. And be sure they know that this assignment should be prioritized above anything else they've got going on."

"Sure thing," Gill agrees and walks outside to make a few calls.

"Do I get a say in any of this?" I ask.

"No," Harlow and Malachi say simultaneously.

Mama and Spooks descend the steps carrying a body bag between the two of them.

"I need to notify her family." I rub my temples to stave off a migraine.

"I'll help with that," Peppermint offers quietly. "I'm used to these kinds of notifications."

I stare at her, silently begging her to elaborate and knowing she won't.

"Thanks."

"Nico, why don't you go grab whatever you need?" Harlow suggests. "We'll salvage what we can down here to help this go a little faster. Then we can all get the hell out of here and figure out what our next move is."

Rage surges through me, tensing every single muscle in my body.

"Our next move is murder."

CHAPTER 13
Peppermint

"MALACHI'S WORRIED ABOUT HIM."

I switch the call to speakerphone and settle deeper into the mattress. The only place Malachi could secure for Nico and me was a one-bedroom apartment. I'm pretty sure it belongs to one of their employees, but I don't particularly care at the moment. Besides, Malachi promised to find something bigger within a few days, but for now, we're stuck.

"Honestly, me too, Har."

Nico placed the call to Bethany's family earlier and they were devastated, to say the least. At one point, I had to take the phone from him because I thought he was gonna break and tell them the truth. I explained to Mr. and Mrs. Sterns that their daughter had been in a car accident and died on impact. The lie made them feel better, even if it did settle in my gut like a lead balloon.

It's weird seeing someone who is usually the upbeat funny one of the group so down. He's been like a zombie since we left his house.

"Is there anything I can do?" Harlow asks, pulling my focus back to the conversation.

"I don't know. Malachi would probably know better than me."

"You don't give yourself enough credit."

"Don't start," I bite out. "I'm too tired for this conversation again."

"Okay."

Shocked by her easy acceptance, I snort. "Either Malachi is waving his dick in front of your face and you're distracted as hell, or I'm going to regret making you wait to say what's on your mind."

"Neither, actually," she says. "I know I'm already on thin ice with you since ordering you to stay with Nico."

"It's fine. You already explained yourself."

She called me while Nico and I strolled through the grocery store randomly tossing junk food into the cart and told me why she made the order.

"Has Malachi figured out our plan yet?" I ask. I was surprised when his reasoning for wanting Nico and me together wasn't as devious as hers.

"I told him," Harlow admits. "He bitched for a minute but then I politely reminded him that he should have expected me to have some tricks up my sleeve. He gets it. And he won't say anything to Nico because he agrees that we're doing the right thing."

"I'm just glad you came to the same conclusion about the message on the wall as I did. There's no way that Nicholi didn't mean that for both Nico and me. I'm one of the ones who got away, *and* I was crucial to taking out his family. He's not going to let that go. And if he's been watching Nico as long as we think he has, he knows how Nico feels about me."

"Right. So it stands to reason that he's more likely to make a move when he can get you both together."

"Exactly. The whole thing with Bethany was child's play for Nicholi. Nico and I are his targets."

"Hey, Mal just walked in so I'm gonna go," Harlow says quickly. "Stay safe."

"Night bitch."

Harlow's laughing is cut off when I disconnect the call. Staring at the ceiling, I debate whether or not to go check on Nico, and concern wins out over self-preservation. I wasn't lying when I told Harlow I was worried about him. He's off, and Nico is never off. I don't like it.

I glance down at the see-through tank and panties I'm wearing and shrug. He was sleeping when I left him in the living room, and he probably still is. No need to get completely dressed.

Nico is sprawled out, one arm flung above his head and one leg hanging over the edge of the couch. His jeans are in a heap on the floor, along with the Henley he was wearing, and his gun and holster rest on the top of the pile. Satisfied that he's okay, I turn to go back to the bedroom, but a deep moan halts me in my tracks.

"I… no… can't… please."

I move closer to the couch to listen to Nico's ramblings, and several more bricks fall away when I see the pain etched in the lines of his face. His head moves back and forth on the cushion and his entire body jerks every few seconds. It doesn't take a genius to figure out what his nightmare is about.

"Nico," I say softly as I crouch next to the couch. I know getting this close probably isn't smart, but I can't help myself. I shake his arm gently. "C'mon, Nico, wake up."

It takes a few more minutes, but Nico comes awake swinging. I dodge out of his way, falling back onto the carpet.

"Whoa, it's just me," I say. Nico stares at me, but his eyes are glazed and unfocused. "Nico, it's me. It's Peppermint." Still, recognition doesn't come. "*Cuore mio*," I whisper.

His eyes clear. "Peppermint?"

I breathe a sigh of relief. "Yeah."

He looks around the room, confusion settling on his features. "What happened? Why are you on the floor?" Nico shoots to his feet. "Did he—"

"Nico, I'm fine," I rush to say as I stand up. I rest my hands on his cheeks and force him to look at me. "I'm good. I promise."

Nico leans into my palm. "I was dreaming, wasn't I?"

"Yeah."

"I'm sorry." He pulls away from me, looking ashamed.

"There's nothing to be sorry about," I assure him. "We all have nightmares sometimes."

"I don't. Or at least, not in a long time."

"It's understandable that today would trigger them."

"Is it?" he counters, heat in his tone. "I've spent years making sure that my childhood never caught up with me, yet here we are. Nicholi's out there somewhere, probably fucking closer than we realize, and I'm in here having a nightmare like a fucking pussy."

"Pity party much?" I tease. He only glares at me so I link my hand with his and drag him down the hall. "We're going to bed. Things will look better in the morning."

"There's something wrong with this picture," he mutters.

"What?"

I close the bedroom door once we're both inside and then steer him to the bed and shove him down.

"You are never the chipper one."

"You're right, I'm not," I agree. "So get some sleep so we can go back to our respective roles. Being upbeat is fucking exhausting."

Finally, Nico smiles. "Yes, ma'am."

He scoots to the opposite side of the mattress and burrows under the covers. I climb in beside him and when he rolls toward me and throws his arm over my stomach, I don't move.

"Peppermint?"

"Yeah?"

"You called me cuore mio."

"Did I?" I grin into the dark.

"You did."

"My bad. It won't happen again."

"It will."

"Go to sleep, Nico."

"Peppermint?"

"What?" I groan.

"You're not wearing any pants." Nico yawns and shifts his arm a little higher. "And I can feel your nipples."

My grin widens, but I harden my tone.

"Go. To. Sleep."

CHAPTER 14
Nico

AWARENESS CREEPS in little by little. The first thing I completely register is the weight covering my stomach and legs. I roll my neck to the side and see Peppermint sound asleep, her hair splayed out on the pillow next to mine. She's facing me, with one hand tucked under her head and the other stretched across my midsection. Her leg is thrown over both of mine but bent at the knee, so her thigh is brushing against my boner.

I close my eyes and savor having her so close. In sleep, she's unguarded in a way I'm sure she hasn't been in her waking moments in years. I know from experience that that is both a blessing and a curse. Hell, the whole reason I'm in bed with her is because I couldn't guard against the nightmares last night.

As much as I'd love to stay in bed with Peppermint and ignore the outside world for a while, I know I need to get up and do some work. Not only did Nicholi trash my house yesterday, but he also ruined my laptop, which held all of my files pertaining to him. Fortunately, I always back up my work to a flash drive which I always keep with me. But I need to get everything loaded onto the new laptop.

When I start to untangle myself from Peppermint, she tightens her hold and pulls me closer.

"Hmm, stay," she mumbles without opening her eyes.

I smile to myself. Fuck, what I wouldn't give for her to always be like this. But then she wouldn't be Peppermint, and Peppermint is pretty perfect just the way she is.

That being said, staying in this position is exquisite torture. Her fingers flex against my skin, barely brushing the flesh, and it teases my senses. My cock jerks against her thigh.

"I'm not sure that's such a good idea," I say, my tone full of lust.

"It's a great idea."

I stare at her, the faint light from the rising sun kissing her cheeks. Her eyes remain closed as she wets her bottom lip with her tongue, eliciting a groan from me.

"*Cuore mio*, the things you do to me."

Rolling to my side, I slide my hand under her tank and skim my fingertips over her stomach until they touch the underside of her breast. Peppermint sighs.

"Open your eyes for me," I instruct in a whisper. When she doesn't, I cup her tit and brush my thumb over the nipple. "I need you to look at me." Peppermint's eyelids slowly rise. "So fucking beautiful."

"I'm scared," she admits, letting her eyes fall closed again.

"Eyes open," I demand as I pinch her nipple. She obeys. "Who do you see?"

"You."

I move my face closer to hers, letting her feel my breath on her skin. "And who am I?"

"Nico."

"Exactly."

I press my mouth to hers, lightly at first. Peppermint stiffens but when I tease the seam of her lips with the tip of my tongue, she moans and deepens the kiss. She darts her tongue out to meet mine, and we vie for dominance. All conscious thought flees my mind as I lose myself in the way she tastes, the sound of her moans. The only thing that matters is the scorching heat moving through my veins. My blood is the gasoline, and Peppermint's kiss is the lit match.

Peppermint moves her hand from my chest to trace a path over my abs, down to the waistband of my boxer briefs. Her fingers work their way under the thin cotton. My cock hardens to a painful degree, and when she brushes her thumb over the tip, I swear the angels dance.

"Fucking hell," I hiss against her lips.

She breaks the kiss, and her eyes lock on mine. She stares so intently that I start to wonder if she's still seeing me. I pull my hand out from under her tank and cup her cheek.

"Who are you seeing, *cuore mio*?"

"You." She wraps her slender fingers around my dick. "Nico."

I grip her wrist and remove her hand so I can shift to straddle her. Her body goes rigid, and her eyes widen. I run my hands up her sides, catching the hem of her tank and pulling it off over her head.

Leaning close to her ear, I whisper, "Say my name again."

"N-Nico," she says with a shiver.

I nip at her earlobe. "Good girl," I praise and then soothe the spot with my tongue. "Mine is the only name that will ever leave your mouth in ecstasy."

Lowering my head, I lap at one nipple while I roll the other between my fingers. Peppermint arches her back seductively.

"Oh, God," she breathes.

I lick a path down her stomach to capture her panties between my teeth and then drag them down her legs as I slide toward the foot of the bed. I spit the flimsy fabric out and make quick work of stripping off my boxer briefs. Peppermint watches my every move with lustful eyes.

"You are so fucking beautiful," I tell her as my gaze travels over her body so I can memorize every last inch. "Perfection."

I lift my knee to the mattress so I can climb on top of her, but she presses a foot to my chest, careful not to hit my stitches.

"If you need me to stop, all you have to do is say so," I tell her. "If you're not ready, that's—"

"I'm ready," she rushes to assure me. "It's just…" Peppermint averts her eyes.

"What is it?"

"I don't know if…" She returns her focus to me and sighs. "Can I be on top?"

She can have anything she fucking wants, as long as she doesn't ask me to stop.

I lunge forward and twist to lie on my back beside her. "You can be wherever you want to be, wherever you need to be."

I tuck my arm under her and pull her so she's straddling my hips. My cock rests against the heat of her pussy and Peppermint rocks her hips. I reach forward to press the pad of my thumb to her clit. She throws her head back at the contact.

"Eyes on me," I command.

Sliding my finger through her damp curls, I tease her entrance while increasing the pressure of my thumb.

"So goddamn wet," I praise. "Wet and ready."

Peppermint frantically shakes her head as her hips continue to undulate, desperately seeking release.

"Are you going to come for me?" I slip a finger into her pussy, then add a second. "You are, aren't you? You're gonna come on my fingers like—"

"Fuuuuuuuck," she cries as her walls spasm, holding my fingers hostage while she rides out the wave of pleasure.

As she comes down from the high only an orgasm can provide, I remove my hand and bring my fingers to my lips.

Her pupils dilate and her nostrils flare when I dip my tongue out and swirl it around my digits to get a taste of her arousal.

"That is so hot," she comments.

Peppermint rises to her knees and centers herself over my shaft. It takes every ounce of willpower I possess not to thrust up and sink into her. My cock is begging for a feel of those aftershocks I feel fluttering through her body.

"Take whatever you need from me," I cajole and grip her hips. "Use me for your pleasure."

Stars flicker in my vision when she drops down and impales herself on me. Her cunt is fucking tight. Combine that with the heat of being inside her and it's like nothing I've ever experienced.

Unable to remain still, I thrust up to meet the demands she's making with her body. My fingers dig into her flesh so hard she'll likely bruise, but I can't stop. If I stop, I fear I'll catapult into blissful oblivion.

Peppermint leans forward and braces her hands on either side of my head. I lift up to kiss her. The added stimulation sends tingles down my spine. Knowing I'm close, I let go of her hip and circle her clit with my thumb.

"Come with me," I demand against her lips.

Thrust after thrust, our bodies expertly play off each other, engaging in a rhythm as old as time. My cock throbs in sync with the fluttering of her inner walls. One second, two seconds... boom!

"Oh sweet Jesus," she cries as we free fall into the ether.

She rides out her orgasm, sucking the life force out of my dick with each pulse. The pleasure lasts longer than ever but is over too fast. Peppermint collapses on top of me in a heap of satisfaction.

I wrap my arms around her and roll us so we're on our sides facing each other. I'm surprised, and elated, when her eyes are open and her lips are curved into a smile.

"I knew we'd be explosive together," I murmur and press a kiss to her forehead.

"Mmm."

Content. That's the only word in the English language to describe how I feel and how she looks.

There's also satisfied, happy, amazing, incredi—

Okay, there are a lot of words, but I'm sticking with content. Because I wasn't sure she'd ever experience that with me, that she would let herself experience it.

Yet here we are.

CHAPTER 15

Peppermint

"LET'S GET STARTED."

Harlow sits in her chair at the head of the table and calls church to order. Malachi and Nico were not happy about being left out of this meeting, but it doesn't pertain to Nicholi, so they need to get over it. We still have a club to run, rescues to complete, and they're not a part of that.

Once she's satisfied that she has everyone's attention, Harlow begins. "I won't keep you long, but Brazen called this morning, and we've got a job," she says, referring to the president of our mother chapter.

"Please tell me this isn't related to Nicholi," Spooks groans.

"It's not. At least, not that we know of."

"Thank fuck."

"Give us the deets, Prez," Mama prompts as she rubs her hands together in excitement. "I'm so in need of shedding a little blood."

I chuckle at her. "We all are."

"Well, you'll get it with this one," Harlow remarks and then turns to our secretary. "Story, can you pull up the pictures Brazen sent?"

"Sure thing." Story opens her laptop and within minutes, a picture of a family is displayed on the wall.

"This is the Bend family," Harlow begins. "Marsha Bend's boss called the cops five days ago when she didn't show up for work. The cops did a welfare check and found the house empty." She nods at Story and the picture changes. "As you can see, there was a struggle, but law enforcement has zero leads. Brazen's contact in the department reached out to her for help."

"I'm surprised that happened so fast," I say.

"Turns out the little girl has a seizure disorder. Her medication was found at the house. Because of her medical condition, the case was assigned to a task force. The problem is, they don't have the connections the DHMC does. Brazen and her girls tracked the family to Atlantic City, and she wants us to go in and get them."

"Where are they?" Giggles asks.

Harlow nods at Story, and the picture changes to a map of a run-down residential neighborhood.

"They're being held here." Harlow points at a spot on the map.

"Is the mission extraction only?"

Harlow grins. "Nope. We have blanket permission to do whatever the hell we want as long as the family is retrieved safely."

Spooks shoots to her feet. "When do we leave?"

"At dark," Harlow responds. "Spooks, you'll have Giggles and Fox to breach the front of the house. I'll have Peppermint and Mama for the back. Story, you'll bring the van and Nate will be with you just in case the girl needs medical attention." She glances around the room. "Any questions?"

When there are none, everyone is excused with orders to meet at the clubhouse at eight tonight. Sounds of the casino filter into the conference room as they leave in a flurry of excitement about the rescue. It hasn't been that long since we've had one, but it always gets the blood pumping.

"Wanna go for a ride?" Harlow asks when we're alone. "I don't know about you, but I need the wind to blow away some of this stress."

"Absolutely."

———

"Remind me to put Vinnie's patch to a vote."

"Shit, she deserves a patch and a spot in the bad bitch hall of fame," I joke. "Anyone who can corral our men like she did when they tried to follow us deserves more than being a prospect has to offer."

Malachi and Nico weren't even sneaky about it. They followed right behind us from the clubhouse to the gate in Malachi's fancy car. I don't know what they were thinking, but it was obviously an exaggeration of their abilities because Vinnie shut that shit down and locked them in.

"Our men?"

"Huh?"

"Our men," Harlow repeats. "You said 'our men'. I wasn't aware that Nico was yours."

"Fuck off," I snap, trying to inject more censure into my tone than I feel.

I'm not ready to admit out loud what my heart has been trying to tell me for a year. I fought Nico tooth and nail, threatened him every chance I got. Which was a lot with all of his texting. But, other than Harlow and spilling blood, he's the only thing that genuinely brought me any happiness since all the shit with Nicholi and the Ricci's was dredged up. My world is dark, but he holds the flashlight and helps me find my way through it.

And the man knows how to use his cock. That certainly doesn't hurt his case any.

"Less girl talk, more action," Spooks says as she steps up next to us.

We parked two blocks away from the house where the Bend family is supposed to be and walked the rest of the way. Story and Nate are sitting in the van right across the street, close by just in case.

"Okay, bitches." Harlow claps her hands together. "We ready?"

Harlow leads the way to the back of the house, leaving me and Mama to follow, while Spooks, Giggles, and Fox make their way onto the porch. Once stationed outside the back door, I glance at my watch and count down the seconds until it reaches nine exactly.

Lifting our feet, Harlow and I simultaneously kick the door, sending it flying off its hinges. We breach the house, weapons drawn. Spooks takes out a guard, slitting his throat in the living room. We move from room to room on the first and second levels, clearing each space. And with each room the family is not in, my disappointment continues.

The last place to look for the Bends is the basement. Harlow gives the hand signal for us to proceed down the steps. I go down first, and the stench that assaults me almost has me tossing my breakfast, lunch, and dinner.

"What the hell?" Mama mutters behind me.

The basement is divided into four cells. Each member of the Bend family is chained to the floor in their own cell. Memories flash of another place where people were chained to the floor. The homemade cells have a bucket, but they don't appear to have been emptied at all.

With my lockpicking skills, it doesn't take long to free them, but it's not going to be easy to get them upstairs. Mrs. Bend is barely conscious, so Spooks lifts her in a fireman's hold and carries her up and out to the van. Mr. Bend is able to walk as long as he's supported. Giggles and Fox lead him out. Harlow cradles the little boy, leaving the little girl for me.

She's currently curled into a ball in the corner and when I step closer to her, she flinches.

"It's okay," I say softly. "I'm gonna get you outta here."

The girl watches me with her sad blue eyes. "My name is Peppermint," I tell her.

"You're Peppermint?" she asks as if she was waiting for me specifically.

Confused by her reaction, I nod.

"He was right."

"Who?"

"The bad man."

A chill races over me.

"And what was he right about, sweetie?"

"He told me you'd come." She scoots toward me. "He said if I gave you a message, you wouldn't hurt me."

Terror settles in my gut. "I'm not going to hurt you even if you don't give me the message. I promise."

The girl seems to consider that and then nods as she reaches her hand into the pocket of her filthy shorts. She pulls out a piece of paper and hands it to me.

"What's this?" I ask, taking it from her.

"The message I'm supposed to give you."

Suddenly, the paper feels like hot coals in my grasp. I tuck it into the inner pocket of my cut and hold my arms out for her. She scrambles into them, her fear seemingly ebbing now that her task is complete.

"Peppermint?"

"Yeah?"

"Thank you for coming to save us."

CHAPTER 16

Nico

"ARE YOU OKAY?"

I stare at the paper in my hands. Peppermint texted me on her way back from their job and asked me to meet her at Devil's Double Down. Malachi got the same request from Harlow and now the four of us are in Harlow's office.

"I don't know how to answer that," I respond honestly.

I read the note again, searching for answers I know won't be there.

P.-

I knew you'd come. You can't resist playing savior. I can't tell you how much I wish the little girl in the basement was you so we could pick up where we left off all those years ago. Just the thought of my mouth on your inner thigh has me throbbing. We're both older now, so there's no reason for you to deny me like you did then.

In case you haven't figured it out, you belong to me. I should've taken you last year when you and that bitch you call a friend killed my father, but the timing wasn't right. It is now.

Be sure to tell that brother of mine that he doesn't have to worry. I'll take care of you for him since he'll be dead. But I do think I'll make him suffer first. I'll send him straight to hell with the image of his twin fucking you imprinted on his gray matter. Won't that be fun?

Until next time, N.

I crumble the paper in my fist and launch it at the wall. Without speaking, Peppermint slides her knife into my hand and nods toward the target by the door.

I throw the knife and she retrieves it for me. I throw, she retrieves. We repeat the process over and over again until my chest is heaving. Malachi and Harlow are standing in the corner, quietly watching, waiting for me to work through my rage.

"Feel better?" Peppermint asks as she hands me the knife again.

I throw the blade as hard as I can and wince when it hits the target. "A little."

"Good. Because we need you to focus and you can't do that when you're spitting mad."

I glance at Malachi. "This has to end."

He nods. "It does." He pushes off the wall and strides toward me. His expression conveys confusion. "Here's what I don't get. The Bends aren't from here or Seattle. How do they factor in?"

"I don't know," I admit, shoving a hand through my hair. "But I promise you I won't stop digging until I do."

"There's something else," Harlow adds. "Nicholi has always been in the skin trade because of the Family. And when we realized he was back in the city, it was because of trafficking victims linked to him. But now he's just killing. Why the switch?"

"Distraction maybe?" Peppermint suggests. "If we're ass deep in murders and watching our own backs, we're not interfering in his money-making activities."

"It's more than that, though." I begin to pace. "I think you're right, but the killing is also a scare tactic. He wants to instill as much fear into us as possible and he thinks that murdering people close to us achieves that."

"It doesn't," Peppermint says vehemently. "It only makes me want to work harder to find him."

"Agreed."

"But that still brings us back to the Bend family," Malachi says. "What the fuck is their connection?"

"As soon as we get back to the apartment, I'll start digging." I address Harlow. "Can you spare Story? She's good with computers and maybe together we'll find something faster."

"Yeah, whatever you need. Do you want her to meet you there tonight, or is tomorrow morning okay?"

"Send her tomorrow," Malachi responds before I can even open my mouth. "I've secured a house for you, so we'll move you there in the morning. You'll have a lot more space to work. There's no sense in doing anything major tonight just to pack it all up and move it in a few hours."

"Okay." I look at Peppermint. "You ready to head out?"

"In a bit. I need to go down and check on the family, make sure they don't need anything."

"Tahiti and Fiona are with them and so is Nate," Harlow says. "You don't have to do anything more."

"I know."

Harlow stares at Peppermint, hard. "Are you sure?"

"It's what I do, Har. I know what they're going through better than anyone." Peppermint rests her hand on Harlow's shoulder. "I'll be fine."

"I'll go with you," I say.

Peppermint glances at me and nods. "Thanks. Appreciate it."

"Why don't we leave them to it and get home?" Malachi suggests to Harlow. "I need to hold you for a while."

Harlow rolls her eyes but leans into Malachi and wraps her arms around him. "Sounds good to me."

"We'll be at the apartment around seven," Malachi says as he guides Harlow out the door. Peppermint and I follow as we're all heading downstairs. "We can help you move whatever shit you have to the new house."

"Perfect. See you then."

We part ways at the bottom of the steps. Peppermint leads me to the elevator that will take us to the underground level of the casino. We ride down in silence and when the doors slide open, she takes a deep breath before stepping out and then another before opening the door to enter the area dedicated to their rescue efforts.

The four family members are sharing two cots: mother and daughter on one and father and son on the other. Emotion clogs my throat at the sight. They're hooked up to IVs, but they couldn't bear to be separated more than they had to be.

"Hey, Pep," Nate greets. "They all just fell asleep. I'm guessing they haven't had much of that in the last few days."

"You wouldn't sleep either if you were kept where they were," she snaps.

"No, of course not."

"Sorry," Peppermint says with a sad smile. "I'm on edge."

"We all are," I reassure her. I rest my hand on the small of her back and she sways slightly. "They're sleeping, Pep. There's nothing more for you to do here."

Peppermint walks away from me to cross the room to where Tahiti and Fiona are sitting at a table.

"How's the chest?" Nate asks.

"Starting to get itchy."

"While you're here, I might as well remove the stitches."

I follow him to his supplies and let him do his thing, but my eyes never leave Peppermint. After a few minutes, Tahiti and Fiona leave and Peppermint joins us.

"Everything okay?" I ask, nodding in the direction of the exit.

"Yeah. I sent them home."

It dawns on me that she plans on sleeping here tonight. I glance at the Bends and can't help but wonder if they realize how lucky they are that Peppermint was part of the team that saved them.

I lift Peppermint's hand and bring it to my lips to press a kiss to the palm.

"I'll set the alarm on my phone for six," I tell her.

CHAPTER 17

Peppermint

ONE MONTH LATER...

"I WISH MY MOM WAS HERE."

I swallow past the lump in my throat and sling my arm around Harlow's shoulders. I wish Velvet was here too. She was only in my life for a few minutes, but I could tell she was a good mom. She was kind to me and not because she had to be. That's just who she was.

Tahiti leans across the bar and grabs Harlow's hand. "I guarantee Velvet is up there watching you, and she'll be throwing a party to celebrate."

"She's right," I chime in. "There is no way Velvet is missing your wedding day."

Harlow swipes her hand under her eyes and sniffles. "Thanks." She groans. "Gah, I hate crying. I'm just glad it's happening now before Giggles does my makeup."

There are moments in a person's life that force them to reflect on the past. This is one of those moments for me. When I was a little girl, I dreamed of fairytales and happily ever afters. Then the Ricci Crime Family entered my world and flipped it on its axis.

My dreams died along with my innocence. I tried to get them back, but every step forward sent me flying face-first into another obstacle. I finally gave up on fighting for the things I lost and focused on the things I still had to gain.

Harlow became the sister I never had and the DHMC morphed into my home. Are there times when I wish things would've been different? Yes. But would I trade what I have now for anything? Not in a million years.

And part of what I have now is Nico. We've settled into a routine over the last month. Story comes to the house almost daily to work with him on tracking Nicholi. Evenings are the hardest moments of the day because that's when Nico gets stuck in his head. Sex helps—when doesn't it?—but I can tell that not finding his brother is wearing him down.

The door between the bar and kitchen swings open, and Fiona steps out carrying plates full of food.

"I've got pancakes," she announces as if we can't see the stacks of them she sets in front of us.

Tahiti and Harlow dig in, but all I can do is stare. My favorite breakfast taunts me from the plate. I know I need to eat, but my stomach is suddenly doing cartwheels.

"What are you waiting for, Pep?" Harlow teases.

Cartwheels turn into backflips and backflips alternate with somersaults. I slap a hand over my mouth and race to the bathroom. I drop to my knees just as the gagging starts and heave the orange juice I had this morning into the toilet.

Sweat beads on my forehead and my stomach starts to cramp. My body continues to make an effort to expel whatever has pissed it off, but there's nothing left.

Cool hands lift my hair off my neck. "I've got you."

Harlow sits on the floor behind me and holds my hair. She rubs circles over my back and whispers soft reassurances that I'm not alone. When I'm done, she helps me to stand. I brace myself on the counter and stare at my reflection. I barely recognize the pale woman looking back at me.

"So…"

I grunt.

"You and Nico?" Harlow prompts.

"What about me and Nico?"

"You slept with him," she states. Her tone is so matter of fact that I want to slap her.

"No." Deny, deny, deny.

I don't know why I've been keeping that information to myself. I tell Harlow everything… well, almost everything. I guess I just wanted something all for me.

"I'm pretty sure the little nugget in your belly is proof to the contrary."

"No. That's not possible."

Her brow arches. "When was your last period?"

"Not that long ago."

I think back to the last time I bought tampons. It was only a couple of days before the night Harlow fractured my cheek. I do the math and—

My jaw drops, and she so very helpfully pushes it back up for me.

Bitch.

"Well, that look tells me everything I need to know."

Harlow grabs a washcloth from under the sink and wets it with cool water. After ringing it out, she presses it to the back of my neck. We lock eyes in the mirror. I deserve to see annoyance staring at me but instead all I see is acceptance, support, and a fuck ton more love than I'm worthy of.

I burst into tears and collapse in a heap on the floor.

"I-I'm s-s-sorry," I stutter between sobs.

"What the hell are you sorry for?" she asks as she sits next to me.

"T-t-this is your d-day."

"And what better gift than finding out I'm gonna be an auntie?" She smiles so big that I immediately cry harder. "That's a good thing, Pep. I'm so fucking happy for you."

"I d-don't know what I'm doing," I wail.

"What parent does?"

Harlow lets me cry until there are no tears left. A round of wet hiccups follow and when those stop, my stomach growls... loudly.

"This whole pregnancy thing is quite the roller coaster ride," she quips. "First you're happy, then you're puking, then bawling and now you're hungry. What's next?"

"Fuck if I know." I climb to my feet, and she does the same. "Dammit."

"What?"

"I'm gonna have to clean up my language, aren't I?"

Harlow doubles over with laughter. I glare at her, failing to see the humor. While she struggles to catch her breath, I brush my teeth with one of the extra toothbrushes we keep a supply of. I toss it in the trash when I'm done so it doesn't get used by someone else.

"You, my friend, are going to be an excellent biker mommy," she says when she sobers. "As for the language?" She shrugs. "Fuck it. They're just words."

"I love you, you know that, right?"

"I do. And I love you too." She links her arm through mine and leads me back toward the main room. "Now, let's go get me married and tell a certain someone that he's going to be a father."

Nico steps around the corner and stops our progress. "Who's going to be a father?"

"Malachi," I spit out without thinking.

Nico's eyes widen and he pulls Harlow in for a hug. "That's great news." Harlow gives me an evil side eye when he steps back. "Congratulations, Har."

"Uh, yeah. Thanks. But can you, um, keep this to yourself?"

"You're not going to tell him?"

"No, I mean, I just..." Harlow groans and looks to me for help.

And like the tongue-tied idiot I've become in the last

ninety seconds, I say the first thing that pops into my addled brain.

"She's going to surprise him after the ceremony. Ya know, when they finally get a minute alone."

Harlow elbows me in the gut, but when she realizes what she just hit, her face pales.

"Oh my God, I'm sorry," she cries.

"Sorry for what?" Nico asks, clearly confused.

"Nothing." I smile brightly. "Did you need something? Why aren't you with Malachi?"

"Oh, right." Nico reaches into his pocket and pulls out a small velvet box which he hands to Harlow. "Malachi asked me to give this to you."

Harlow holds the box to her chest. "And now you have so you should go."

"Okay." Nico presses a quick kiss on my cheek. "See you soon."

"Yep. Soon."

He stares at us, his gaze darting back and forth for a few more seconds before turning and walking away. I'm pretty sure he mutters something about weddings and hormonal women, but I'm too stunned by what just happened to give a shit.

"Are you out of your fucking mind?" Harlow shouts after Nico exits the clubhouse. "Now what am I supposed to do? I can't tell Malachi I'm pregnant because I'm NOT!"

"You really shouldn't get worked up, Har." I try to keep my tone soothing, but it only comes out squeaky. I fucked up. I fucked up big time.

Harlow takes several deep breaths. "Okay. I'm calm. I know what to do."

"What?"

"Lie through my goddamn teeth. I'll tell Malachi I thought I was pregnant because I was late but then I took a test today and it was negative." Her words are rushed, almost as if she doesn't believe the lie will work.

"That'll work," I say weakly. "Right?"

Harlow bends and lifts my shirt slightly to kiss my stomach.

"I'm sorry for the love tap, little nugget," she says. When she stands, she leans in to hug me but moves her mouth to my ear.

"I didn't want the kid to hear, but this better fucking work, Pep."

CHAPTER 18
Nico

"THE CEREMONY WAS BEAUTIFUL."

Peppermint nods but doesn't take her eyes off the steak knife she's been twirling in her fingers for the last ten minutes. The crowd at the clubhouse continues to grow as the reception carries on around us. Malachi and Harlow were married at a small church, but that was the extent of Harlow's giving in to tradition.

"I especially enjoyed the elephant Harlow and Malachi rode back to the clubhouse."

"Uh huh."

"Okay, that's it." I yank the knife out of her hand and slam it onto the table. "What is going on with you?"

"Nothing."

"You just agreed with me about an elephant the bride and groom rode after the ceremony."

She looks at me incredulously. "There wasn't an elephant."

"Exactly." I cup her cheek. "Is this about Harlow being pregnant?"

"What? Why would you think that?"

I shrug. Why do women have to be so complicated?

"I don't know. I mean, we've never talked about kids or a future. Maybe you're jealous or sad or maybe you can't have kids and that has you distracted. I don't know why you'd be upset about it, and I don't know why you're so in your head. That's kinda why I'm asking."

When she simply stares at me like I've grown a second nose, my temper flares.

"Ya know what, forget it." I rise from the table and push my chair in. "We've come a long way, you and me, but if you want to start shutting me out again, fine. Come find me when you change your mind."

I stalk away, angry at myself and angry at Peppermint. Since the first night we slept together, things between us have been good. Better than good, actually. I don't know exactly what changed, but Peppermint seemed to accept that we belong together, acted as if she wanted it as much as I do.

Was I wrong?

I lift my hand to Fiona, who's bartending as usual, and signal that I want a beer. Harlow offered to give her the night off so she could enjoy the reception, but Fiona was having none of it. She told her prez and Malachi to consider it a wedding gift from her and Coast.

I lift the frosty bottle she sets on the bar for me but before I can take a pull, I'm spun around and lose my grip. The beer crashes to the floor and breaks, the liquid splashing onto my pants.

"What the hell?" I snap at Malachi, the asshole who ruined my attempt at numbing the hurt.

Malachi holds his hands up. "Whoa, sorry. You were racing over here like there was a fire that needed pissed on. Just wanted to make sure everything was okay."

"Yeah." I force a smile and slap his chest. "It's your wedding day, man. Of course everything is okay."

Malachi grins. "Did you get a look at that dress, Nico? Fuck, I am one lucky bastard."

"Harlow looked incredible. And the necklace you got her was the perfect addition."

"Never in a million years did I think I'd be marrying a woman who is so happy about a hatchet pendant that I get laid for it."

A tap on my back has me turning around. Fiona hands me another beer.

"Thanks, Fi."

"Dude, nobody calls my woman Fi but me," Coast growls from behind her.

"Right. Sorry."

I down half the bottle before facing Malachi again. "I'm happy for you, Mal. If anyone deserves a marriage and a kid on the way, it's you."

"If you'd have asked me two years ago what I thought about Harlow, I'd have given you a list of reasons why I hated her. But now? I can't imagine—" He presses his lips together for a moment and then tilts his head. "Wait a sec. What did you say?"

"Just that I'm happy for you. Both of you."

"Yeah, yeah, I got that part." He nods slowly. "But the other thing… the part about a kid on the way?"

"Oh, right. Congratulations. I'm sorry I knew before you, but I overheard—"

Malachi grabs my wrist and yanks me away from the bar.

"What are you doing?"

He doesn't answer. He drags me through the crowd of drunk guests doing the Cha Cha Slide, ignoring all the hands that try to grab him to dance. We reach the hall, and he stops to turn around and scan the crowd.

"Harlow," he shouts to be heard over the music. I follow his gaze and see her head pop up from a conversation she's having. "Meeting room. Now!"

Malachi shoves me into the room, causing me to stumble.

"What the fuck, man?" I gripe.

"What is your problem?" Harlow demands when she walks in shortly after us.

"Someone better start talking," Malachi seethes, glaring at both of us.

"Why aren't you happy about this?" I ask, starting to get pissed off.

More like jealous as fuck that he's getting the life you want.

"Mal, what is he talking about? Why aren't you happy?"

"I am happy," he snaps. "But I'd be happier if it had been my *wife* who told me I'm going to be a daddy."

"Oh," she says, and then her eyes widen comically. "Oh."

"Damn, Harlow, I'm sorry. I thought you told him. You said you were going to tell him after the ceremony."

"No, no I didn't," she says. Her face scrunches up.

"Yes, you did. You said—"

"*I* didn't say anything," she corrects. "Peppermint did most of the talking, if you'll recall."

"Okay, fine. Peppermint said it. It hardly matters."

"Will someone please fucking explain what is going on before I have a goddamn heart attack?" Malachi shouts.

Harlow takes a deep breath and lifts Malachi's hands into hers. "Mal, I love you. And I want to have babies with you… someday."

"Someday is here," I remind her.

"It is," she agrees. "But not for me and Malachi."

"Wait. So you're not pregnant?" Malachi asks.

"No, I'm not. But I'm all for practicing as often as it takes to get the whole baby making process just right."

"But if you're not pregnant, what was this morning all about? Who were you and Peppermint talking about being a father?"

Harlow drops one of Malachi's hands to pick up one of mine.

"Nico, use that beautiful brain of yours," she says. "If we weren't talking about me and Malachi, who else co—"

Realization dawns. "No."

"Yeah."

"She's on the pill. She said she's on the pill."

"Looks like you've got strong swimmers," Malachi jokes.

Delight and irritation wage a war against each other in my soul. I'm gonna be a father. Holy shit. But the mother couldn't even bring herself to tell me. Son of a bitch.

Irritation wins, spurring me into action. I race out of the room, ignoring Malachi and Harlow calling after me to stop. The reception remains in full swing, which is good. Because something tells me that carrying Peppermint out of here caveman style is going to piss her off. The less of a scene I create, the better for me later.

Peppermint is still sitting at the table, the knife back in her hand. She's alone, and the black streaks down her cheeks tell me she's been crying. My heart bleeds at the sight, and my irritation dies a quick death. I force myself to slow down, to keep my emotions in check because something tells me she needs me to be strong right now, even if I'm feeling anything but.

When I reach the table, I make a point to gently touch her shoulder so as not to scare her. She flinches, but when her eyes land on me, her body relaxes.

"I thought you left."

I crouch down in front of her. "I'll never leave you, *cuore mio*."

"I wouldn't blame you if you did."

I take the knife from her hand and set it on the table. As I stand, I shift so I can lift her in my arms.

"What are you doing?" she screeches.

"Taking you home."

"I can't leave. They haven't even cut the cake yet."

"Harlow will understand."

I kick the door open and step out into the night air.

Peppermint shivers in my arms so I hold her a little closer, a little tighter.

"I was planning on staying here tonight," she reminds me.

"I know. The plan changed."

"I don't understand," she argues. "Why did it change?"

When I reach my car, I set her on her feet so I can open the passenger door. I urge her inside the vehicle and then lean in to buckle her seatbelt. As I'm scooting back out, Peppermint grabs my arm.

"Nico, why did the plan change?"

I really didn't want to get into this here. It would be so much easier to handle her unpredictability out of earshot of so many people. But we don't always get what we want.

"It changed because I refuse to let the mother of my child sleep in a glorified frat house while drunk asshats party directly below her bedroom."

CHAPTER 19
Peppermint

THE DRIVE to the house is tense, to say the least. We're only five minutes away when I decide to text Harlow.

> **Me: You prob noticed we left. Nico's really mad. I'm sorry, Har. This was your day and I ruined it.**

I stare out the window at the trees passing us by. I'd much rather be on my Harley, especially when my whole being feels so out of whack, but Nico refused to let me out of his car. My phone dings with a text.

> **Harlow: You didn't ruin anything. I'm married to Malachi and that was kinda the only goal today. Talk to him, give him a chance, P. Nico is just hurt right now.**

> **Me: Love you, Mrs. Ricci.**

> **Harlow: Love ya back, future Mrs. Ricci.**

> **Me: Fuck off.**

I twist to look at Nico when the vehicle stops. He shifts into park and depresses the button to shut the garage door.

"We're home," he says unnecessarily.

"I know."

"Looks like the security team is in place for the night."

Malachi has insisted the team remain on duty any time we're at the house, despite having a state-of-the-art security system installed. It pissed me off at first, but now, with more than just myself and Nico to think about, it's… comforting.

"That's good."

"C'mon, let's get inside."

Nico gets out of the car and comes around to open my door. He takes my hand and tucks it under his arm. It hits me just now: I've changed. Where before I would have balked at chivalry, now I welcome it. I would have sliced a fucker up for daring to treat me like I can't do things for myself.

Nico has changed me. I wait for the panic to crawl up my spine, but it doesn't.

The door lock engaging startles me, and I flinch.

"What is it?" Nico asks, concern etched in his expression.

"Nothing."

Nico tosses his keys into the bowl on the kitchen counter and kicks off his shoes. He kneels down in front of me and slowly, reverently, takes my heels off, kissing the arches of my feet after each one.

As he stands, he trails his fingertips up the insides of my legs, hiking my dress up as he does. When the material bunches around my waist, he pushes me back toward the wall with his hips and lifts the dress over my head. After dropping it to the floor, he unhooks the front closure of my lace bra and pushes the straps off my shoulders.

"I'm going to love on every inch of your body, right here against the wall," he growls. "And when I'm done, I'm going to carry you upstairs and draw you a bath, which we're both going to enjoy."

"Mmm," I purr, my thighs clenching at the thought.

He nibbles on my bottom lip, then soothes the sting with his tongue. Nico slides his hands into the waistband of my thong and shoves the lace over my hips. He drags them down my legs, his mouth following in their wake. He repeats his path from earlier, stopping at the apex of my thighs.

Burying his nose in my curls, he breathes in deeply. "Your smell does wicked things to me, *cuore mio*."

I try to force myself closer to his mouth, but he tsks and grips my hips to hold me in place.

"Stand there and be patient," he commands, his tone husky.

"I can't," I cry. "I need you."

"I know you do. Trust me to give you what you need."

Nico flattens his tongue on my clit, causing me to buck wildly. He expertly works the bundle of nerves until I'm barely able to hold myself upright. My legs shake and my knees buckle, but he doesn't let me fall.

Instead, he shoves two fingers into my pussy, and the added sensation sends me flying high. I moan out my release until I worry my voice will be lost to the pleasure. My muscles relax, more and more as I float back down to Earth, but still, Nico doesn't completely stop.

He keeps his tongue flattened against my skin as he stands, licking my arousal up my body to my lips. I suck his tongue into my mouth to deepen the kiss, primal in my need to taste what he does to me.

"You taste so good," he murmurs against my lips.

Nico slides his wet fingers in to replace his tongue, and I lick them clean. My eyes lock on his while I savor my juices and my hands work the buttons on his shirt and then his pants. I clumsily strip him, grateful when his cock springs free between us.

I jump up, giving Nico no choice but to catch me. I wrap

my legs around his waist and, using the wall as leverage, maneuver until I'm able to impale myself on his dick. Nico rests his forehead against mine.

"This wasn't the plan," he says, his jaw tight.

"Seems we're both good at changing the plan."

Nico surges inside of me, his hips flying and pinning me to the wall. His thrusts are brutal and in complete contrast to the way he nuzzles my cheek with his nose. Nico is a hard man, but soft when it matters.

I'm lost in the movement, in the blinding pleasure swirling through my system. I'm lost to him. And I don't ever want to be fucking found.

Nico moves his hand between us to rub my clit, and the contact sends me soaring. My pussy contracts around him, taking from his cock whatever it wants. He thrusts one time, two times, and his body jerks with his release.

Panting, neither of us move. I lean my head against the wall and run my fingers through his damp hair. His cock slides out, and cum runs down my thighs.

"You are truly *cuore mio*," he whispers.

My lips tip into a smile. "I love you too."

Nico rears back. "What?"

I lift my head so I can look him in the eyes. "I didn't want to. I made no bones about that. But somewhere between the daily morning texts and hearing you call me the mother of your child, it happened. It's pointless to deny it. And honestly, I'm tired of fighting it."

"You love me?"

I press a kiss to his lips and nod. "Yes, Nico, I love you."

Tears gather in his eyes and when one spills over, I brush it away. Without a word, Nico carries me to the master bathroom where he sets me on my feet. After starting the bath water, he lifts me back into his arms and steps over the ledge to sink down into the tub.

Still, no words are spoken. Part of me worries that I fucked up, that I said the wrong thing, but then he touches me, cares for me, and all worry fades away. The water cools, so we get out and Nico dries me with a towel. After blow drying my hair for me, he carries me to the bed where he tucks us both under the covers.

"I love you too, Peppermint."

———

"Rise and shine."

I fling my arm over my eyes to block out the light. I'm exhausted and want nothing more than to stay under the covers.

"No," I grumble. "No rise and no shine."

"Yes," Nico says flatly. "I even made your favorite breakfast."

A weight settles above me, and the scent of pancakes and syrup assaults my senses. My eyes fly open, and I shove the tray of food away so I can rush to the bathroom. I drop to the tile floor with seconds to spare before my stomach revolts.

Much like Harlow did yesterday, Nico settles behind me and holds my hair back. I don't think there's much to worry about though because there is nothing in my stomach to throw up. Dry heaves wrack my body for what feels like hours.

"If this is what we're in store for, we're stopping at one child," he says hotly when I lean against his chest. "I can't stand watching you suffer."

"You talk as if more children are a given." Exasperation fills my tone. "Nico, we weren't expecting this one."

"No, we weren't," he agrees. "And now that we're talking about it, we really do need to talk about it."

I roll my eyes. He's right, we do, but leave it to a man to say we need to do something we're already doing.

"Okay." I scoot forward. "But first, breakfast. I'm starving."

"You're…" Nico shakes his head as he pulls me to my feet. "Ya know what, never mind."

I stare longingly at the pancakes on the bedroom floor. "Why does little nugget have to hate what I love?" I complain.

"Little nugget?"

I shrug. "That's what Harlow was calling it."

"It?"

"Esmerelda," I offer, laughter in my tone. "Byron, Starla… oh, I know! McLovin." I rub a hand over my flat stomach as I walk to the kitchen. "Hey there, McLovin," I croon.

"You're impossible," Nico pouts from behind me.

"Yet you love me," I tease. "Go figure."

"Life will certainly never be dull."

"You were worried about that?"

Nico laughs as he shakes his head. "No. Not even a little bit."

"Oooh, do we have bacon?" I open the fridge and start digging around. I find a bag of baby carrots and grab one. "Or what about pepper jack cheese?" I ask around a mouthful of the orange veggie. "I could go for a cheese omelet."

"Sit down and I'll fix you something," he commands, pulling me away from the fridge and pushing me down into a dining chair.

"So bossy."

"I think you secretly like being bossed around."

"Maybe. But you will take that information to your grave unless you want to be introduced to your final resting place at a young age."

"Fair enough."

Nico focuses on fixing us both breakfast while I sit and contemplate what to say. It's easy to joke with him, and he's great about playing along, but I know there are things we actually have to discuss.

One of us has to dive in, and I decide it's going to be me.

"I'm scared."

Nico turns from the stove to look at me. "About?"

"Everything," I admit. "But mostly about being a parent."

"You'll be an amazing mom."

"Nico, I haven't even taken a pregnancy test yet, that's how stupid I am about all this. I mean, I know I need to, but I started puking yesterday, and Harlow said I was pregnant, and I went along with it because pregnant chicks puke, right?" I suck in a breath.

Nico sets a plate of food in front of me, and I relax when my stomach doesn't protest the smell.

"We'll have Nate do a blood test tomorrow, just to be sure."

"That's it?" I ask, not giving a shit that my mouth is full of eggs. "You're not mad?"

"Why would I be mad? You got caught up in the moment, and then there's the fact that it was Harlow and Malachi's wedding day." Nico shrugs as he sits in the chair across from me. "I'm guessing, based on the vomiting, the exhaustion, and the, uh…" He points his fork at my plate. "The appetite, you're pregnant. And if we're wrong, then something else is going on and we'll figure it out."

"Oh."

That was easy.

"Ya know," he begins. "We've never talked about your family. Tell me about them."

"The DHMC is my family.'

"Yeah, but your biological family. You've got a mom and dad, right?"

"You mean you haven't researched the shit out of my life yet?" I snark. I don't like to talk about my family. I know I need to, especially since that's causing the majority of my fear, but I don't want to.

"Nope. I knew what I needed to know. The rest I wanted to learn from you, not the internet." He takes another bite, swallows. "So, your family?"

I take a deep breath. It's now or never.

"I was an only child. My parents doted on me. And then I was kidnapped," I say flatly.

"I'm sorry."

"It's not your sin to apologize or atone for, Nico." I lean back in my chair, my plate now empty. "After Velvet, Harlow's mom, and DHMC rescued me, I was brought to the casino, the basement. I woke up on a cot, confused, my mind fuzzy from the drugs." When Nico winces, I reach across the table and grab his hand. "It's not your fault. Anyway, Velvet went back, and I never saw her again. But Harlow was there, always. We called my family." I sigh, remembering. "I was so excited because I thought they'd come get me as fast as they could. But that's not what happened."

Nico rises from the table and carries our dishes to the sink. He rinses them but looks over his shoulder. "What did happen?"

Pain lances my heart. I thought I'd gotten over it, the rejection, the grief, but I guess I haven't. Maybe I never will.

"My dad answered the phone. At first, he sounded happy to hear from me. He asked me about what happened, and I told him. Every single detail. By the time I was done, he was crying. That's when my mom spoke for the first time during the call. She very politely said that she wasn't sure who I was, but that she and her husband didn't have a daughter, that their daughter died the night she was kidnapped. I begged her to stop lying, to recognize that I was her little girl, but it didn't matter. The last words she spoke to me were 'I hope you're able to find people to love your damaged soul."

"Jesus."

"Harlow was screaming into the phone as my mother hung up. I was sobbing. From that moment on, Harlow became my family."

"We're a pair, aren't we?"

"Yeah, but we're a perfect pair."

CHAPTER 20

Nico

"ARE YOU SURE ABOUT THIS?"

I nod at Story. She arrived a few hours ago, but I just got up the nerve to ask her for this favor. I don't know if it's the right thing to do or not, but I have to try. If for no other reason than to help Peppermint.

"Just keep it to yourself, please."

"Nico, I might need to bring Harlow in on this one. If shit goes south, and it often does with our crew, P's gonna need her."

I sigh. She's right. "Fine. But only Harlow."

"Got it."

We spend the next two hours doing what we do every day: digging as deep as we can into anything that could lead us to Nicholi. We have yet to connect the Bends to any of this, and my twisted brother seems to have gone underground. Not that I'm complaining, but it doesn't quite sit right.

Nicholi doesn't run and hide, he creates chaos.

"Hey Story."

I turn toward the door and whistle at Peppermint as she walks in.

"Hey P," she responds without looking away from the computer.

"I see you're still hard at work, so I won't keep you. I've gotta run to the casino for a bit, check in with the staff, and then I'm meeting Nate at the clubhouse so he can do a blood draw."

"I don't like you going out alone," I remind her.

"Which is why two of the security team from out front will follow me the entire time… like a child."

"Is Gill going, or will he still be here?" I much prefer he's with her rather than me. She's carrying precious cargo after all.

Peppermint rolls her eyes. "I'll take him with me if that will make you feel better."

"It will."

"Okay."

She pecks me on the lips and then sashays out of the room. I hate to see her leave, but fuck I love watching her go.

Corny fucker.

"I love you," I call out to her.

"Love you too," she hollers.

"Is this what it's going to be like from now on?" Story asks. "Because if it is, I'm gonna stay and work at the club-house from now on. I don't need any lovey dovey crap rubbing off on me."

"We'll try to reign it in when you're around," I say flatly.

"Thanks," she quips.

Two hours later, I stand to stretch. "I'm gonna grab some-thing to drink. Can I get you anything?"

With her nose still buried in her laptop, Story shakes her head. Her fingers are flying over the keyboard. I hurry to the kitchen to grab a bottled water and snag a bag of chips on my way back through.

"Son of a bitch!"

I break out in a run at Story's shout. Sliding on the hardwood floor, I round the corner into the office.

"What? What's wrong?"

Story looks at me with a stunned expression. "I did it."

"Did what?"

"Found the connection."

I step up next to her so she can show me what she found.

"See," she says and points to her screen. "So, we started with the Bend family. I started with her boss, but quickly dismissed him. But we've been coming up empty for a month now, so I decided to go back to him. Something just wasn't sitting right with me."

"Okay, I'm following so far." *I think.*

"I was able to find where the boss's name on paper doesn't match the actual person. He was using a fake name."

"Okay, still following. How does finding that out connect the Bends to Nicholi?"

"Right here." She slides her finger down the screen a little. "There are hundreds of phone calls between the boss and Nicholi over the years. Probably thousands."

"Who the fuck is Marsha Bend's boss?"

"On paper, Jack Johnson. Boring, right?" I nod and motion for her to continue. She opens a different window on her screen, and my stomach drops. "Meet Yanni D'Amico, a.k.a. Jack Johnson."

"I need to call Malachi," I say absently.

"I don't think that's such a good idea. He's probably balls deep in his wife right about now. And I don't know about you, but I do not want to be on the receiving end of the damage Harlow can do with a hatchet." She waves her hand dismissively. "Besides, they'll be home in a few days. It's taken us this long. A few days won't hurt anything."

"Story, I wish you were right about that. But with Yanni D'Amico, a few days can change everything."

Memories flash, bits and pieces of time that I wish I could

forget. I'm thrown back to that dirty motel room on the outskirts of Philadelphia.

"Wider."

I spread my legs as wide as I can and focus on the dingy brown carpet. It's lucky for Yanni that my blood hasn't been too noticeable on the ratty shag. Not so lucky for me. My muscles ache, and my back is on fire. I jerk when the whip slices across my flesh for the fifth time... today.

Father banished me four days ago. Yanni had been instructed to take me somewhere to heal from the wounds inflicted by my father as punishment. Then he's to take me to Evergreen Boys Academy.

This motel is the second one we've been to and we're only a couple of hours from home. Or what used to be my home.

"I'll turn you into a man. No fucking academy can do what I can."

"Yes, sir," I say as tears well in my eyes. I blink them back because if he sees them, he'll beat me harder.

Yanni whips me three more times, then shoves me toward the bathroom. "Go clean yourself up. You look disgusting."

I do as he says, leaving the door open. That's another infraction that makes the beatings worse. After I towel dry myself off, I go straight to the bed furthest from the door. I silently pray that Yanni stays away tonight, but when the mattress dips with his weight, I know God isn't listening. It seems he never does.

"Take the shorts off," Yanni demands.

I force my mind to take me somewhere else, somewhere warm. I'm always cold anymore, so warm sounds nice. I'm on the beach, and a pretty girl is walking toward me. I recognize her, she's the one I hope got saved. I open my mouth to call out her name, but no words come out. I don't know her name.

"Go to sleep," Yanni barks, yanking me back to the present.

He rolls away from me. I count the seconds while I wait for him to fall asleep. When he begins to snore, I creep out of bed and go clean myself up... again. I think about trying to escape, but fear keeps me from doing it.

If I'd have known that there were eight more motels and count-less beatings between that motel and Washington, I'd have run. If I'd have known that he would violate me every single night along that journey, I'd have run.

Fear be damned.

The sting of a palm across my cheek registers, and I'm dragged back to reality.

"What the hell was that?" Story demands. "Where the fuck did you just go?"

I blink to clear my head, and the room slowly comes back to focus.

"I need to call Malachi."

"I'm way ahead of you," she says and shakes her cell in front of my face. "You were wiggin' out, so I called him."

"Nico, is it true?" Malachi's voice comes through the speaker.

"I wish it wasn't."

"Yanni's back?" he asks, sounding as if he's trying to garner a different answer from me.

"Yeah, Mal. Yanni D'Amico is back."

CHAPTER 21

Peppermint

"CONGRATULATIONS."

I absently rub the crook of my arm where Nate drew blood for the pregnancy test. My stomach has been in knots waiting for the results but luckily for me, the good doc has a contact at the lab, and he had them rush it. It still took several hours, but now the wait is over.

"Thanks."

Nate looks at me with concern in his eyes. "Is this not a good thing?"

"What?"

"It's just…" He shrugs. "You don't seem happy about it."

"Oh, no, I'm happy. It's a shock for sure, but a good one."

"Good." Nate hands me a business card. "I sent a referral to Dr. Herra for your prenatal care. You're first appointment is in two weeks."

"I appreciate it."

"Don't mention it."

The door to the clubhouse flies open, drawing our attention. Nico strides in, his expression furious, and Story is right behind him.

"I thought I was meeting you at home?" I call out to him.

Nico closes the distance between us and wraps me up in a hug. When he finally lets go, he turns to Nate.

"What's the word, Doc?"

"Congrats, Dad," Nate replies with a grin.

Nico lifts me off my feet and spins me around. As much as I love being in his arms, little nugget isn't a fan of spinning. And Nico still hasn't answered my question.

"Put me down," I complain.

"Sorry," Nico says when he sets me on my feet. "I couldn't help it. I'm so fucking happy."

"Great, me too. But a minute ago you looked like you wanted to kill someone with your bare hands."

"That's because he does," Story comments, almost as if she's annoyed by it. "I'm gonna go get some sleep. Once Harlow and Malachi are back in the morning, there won't be much time for that."

Story walks away, toward the stairs to go up to her room. I stare at Nico, silently commanding him to tell me what the fuck is going on.

"Why are Harlow and Malachi coming home in the morning? They're on their honeymoon!"

Nico suddenly looks uncomfortable. He darts his gaze everywhere but at me.

"Nico," I grind out.

"Nate, thanks for doing the blood test," Nico says and shakes the doctor's hand. "But you can head on home."

"Sure thing," Nate says.

"Nico, what is going on?" I ask as I drag him to the table at the back of the main room.

"Story did it," he says flatly. "She connected the dots between the Bend family and Nicholi."

"That's great."

"It is."

"Why do I get the feeling that it's not great?" I narrow my eyes. "What's the connection?"

"Marsha Bend's boss."

"I don't understand."

Nico takes his cell phone out of his jacket pocket and taps the screen a few times before turning it around so I can see.

"Recognize him?"

"Of course I do," I snap. "But Yanni's dead. He was taken out last year when Malachi and Gill wiped the town clean of any connection to the Family."

Nico reaches for my hand, but when I pull away, he leans back and sighs. "That's what we thought."

"I'm not following."

I am following, but I'm praying I'm wrong, praying he's wrong. Knowing that Nicholi is still out there is bad enough. Add Yanni into the mix, and everything becomes unbearable.

"Yanni is Marsha's boss."

Nico watches me carefully for my reaction. I don't know if he expects me to flip out or crumble, but he gets neither because all I am is numb.

"That's…" I shake my head. "No."

Nico nods. "Yes. Story uncovered communication between Yanni and Nicholi. It seems Yanni has set up a new trafficking system near your mother chapter. He *gifted* the Bend family to Nicholi as a way to entice my brother into the new business. I guess he thought if he helped Nicholi on his quest to destroy us, Nicholi would join him. With their combined experience, they could take over the skin trade."

"This can't be happening." I stand but have to grip the edge of the table to steady myself. "Not now. Nicholi's been quiet lately. I thought… I was hoping he'd just disappeared."

"Ah, Pep, you know that wasn't going to happen."

Nico comes around the table and wraps his arms around me from behind, resting his chin on my shoulder.

"I'm so sorry," he says. "I wish this wasn't happening, but it is." Nico buries his face in my neck. "We'll get them, I promise you. This world will be free of them by the time our baby becomes a part of it."

"You don't know that. You can't promise that," I argue, pulling out of his hold. I turn to face him. "I, uh... I just need a little time to process this. You should go home."

Hurt flashes in Nico's eyes, but I don't have it in me to soothe him right now. "If that's what you want," he says.

"I don't want any of this, Nico. But the cards have been dealt, and I need to figure out how to play the hand."

I walk away from him and up the stairs to my room. Locking the door behind me, I lean back and blow out a breath. I am no stranger to the fight or flight response, and I've spent years relying on fight, perfecting it. But right now, in this moment, all that I want is to flee. Fast and so fucking far.

I crawl under the blanket on my bed and curl up in the fetal position. It crosses my mind that shutting Nico out is going to come back and bite me in the ass, but I shove the thought aside. Morning is soon enough to deal with that.

_____

Ping.

Ping.

I roll away from the insistent beeping of notifications on my cell.

Ping.

"Leave me alone," I shout into the pillow.

Ping.

"Son of a…" I blindly reach behind me for the device. "Fine, you win."

I lift the screen to my face and see several text notifications from Nico. I also see it's only seven in the morning, which is too early to deal with anything without coffee.

"Shit," I mutter when I remember I can't have coffee. Not

while I'm pregnant. I flatten my hand on my stomach. "I hope you appreciate how difficult this is for mommy, little nugget."

Sitting up, I read the texts.

Nico: Good morning, cuore mio.

Nico: I miss you.

Nico: How'd you sleep?

Nico: How's the tummy today?

Despite everything, these texts have the same effect they always do. I smile, feeling a little lighter than I did last night. I throw the blanket off me and stand. It's time to go home and face the music. I tap out a reply.

Me: Morning. I miss you too. Coming home.

Ping.

I stare at the door. That notification didn't come from my phone, but it was close.

He didn't.

I cross the room to yank open the door and freeze.

Oh yes, he did.

"Nico, what are you doing?" I ask.

He stands up and steps toward me. "You stayed here, so I stayed here." The statement is so simple, so matter of fact, like I should have known that's what he was going to do.

"Where did you sleep?"

He shrugs. "Managed a little out here."

"On the floor?" I ask incredulously.

"Like I said, you were here."

"You're crazy, you know that?"

"Maybe. But I don't really give a fuck. I need to know

you're safe, always. I can't make sure of that if I'm some-where else."

"No, I guess you can't," I say. "But I'll remind you, I can take care of myself."

"Yes, you can. But you don't have to."

Nico frames my face with his hands and gently backs me into the room. He doesn't stop until I bump into the bed.

"I'm tired, Pep," he says, and as if to prove his point, he yawns. "Whaddya say we sleep until Harlow and Malachi get here?"

"Have you heard from them?"

"Yeah. They should be here in a few hours."

"Okay." I tug him onto the mattress and scoot so my back is to his front. "Let's sleep."

CHAPTER 22

Nico

"YOU READY FOR THIS?"

I twist away from the window to look at Malachi. We're sitting in front of the building Yanni lives in. It's more rundown than I was expecting. Maybe human trafficking doesn't pay like it used to.

"Are you?" I counter.

The original plan was for Peppermint and Harlow to come with us, but I couldn't let that happen. I need to face my demons without having to worry about those two. Those three if you count the baby. So, Malachi and I left before they woke up.

I left a note for Peppermint, but I'm not stupid enough to think that that is sufficient. It's not. I'll take the consequences and be content in the knowledge that she is safe.

"Let's do this."

We exit the vehicle, purpose in our movements. I sling my bag over my shoulder and whistle as we walk inside. Yanni's apartment is on the third floor, and the elevator is broken so we take the stairs.

"I'm surprised he's living in a place like this," Malachi comments.

I think back to all the seedy motels Yanni took me to. "It suits him."

"He's fallen pretty far since the Family. Father and Uncle would never have allowed their man to live like this."

"You'd be surprised at what they would allow," I mutter.

Malachi looks over his shoulder at me as we reach the door for the third floor. "What do you mean?"

Malachi isn't stupid. He has to be aware that there are things he doesn't know. But he'll find out soon enough.

"Nothing," I tell him. "But remember, when we get in there, he's mine. I don't care if you fuck with him, but I get his last breath."

"I remember."

We reach Yanni's apartment, and I knock on the door. Adrenaline is flowing rapidly through my veins. My heart is hammering against my ribs, and my nerve endings buzz with anticipation.

The door swings open and then he's there. Yanni D'Amico is not the man I remember, the man who haunts me. He doesn't even resemble the most current pictures Story found of him.

The puzzle pieces start falling into place, clicking and locking to create a full picture.

Yanni isn't the mastermind we've been giving him credit for. No, the only reason he wants Nicholi is because he can't fucking hack it on his own. He needs the Ricci name to climb to the top.

He's sure got a lot of people fooled though.

"Yanni, my man," I say jovially, laughing at his look of horror at Malachi and me being on his proverbial doorstep. "Long time, no see."

"Nicholi?" There's hope in his tone… hope with a dash of panic that I am indeed the twin he does *not* want to see.

"Guess again."

I flatten my hand on his chest and shove him inside. He

stumbles, but quickly rights himself. I drop my bag to the floor next to me, and Malachi locks the door behind us, the click of it engaging causing Yanni to flinch.

"Wh-what are you doing here?" he stutters.

I tilt my head and grin. "Can't an old friend just stop by for a chat?"

"And here I thought you weren't in a chatting mood," Malachi comments.

"I'm not," I assure him. "But I'm trying to be a polite house guest."

"Oh, right. Makes sense." He grins at Yanni. "Wouldn't want to sully the Ricci name by being rude."

"Exactly. Unfortunately, Yanni here is being a horrible host. He hasn't even offered us a drink yet."

"I don't know about you, but I could go for a shot of whiskey."

"That does sound good."

"I've got whiskey if you want it," Yanni rushes to assure us.

Malachi lands a right hook to his face, and his head snaps to the side. I hold onto Yanni to keep him upright and smirk at the blood gushing from his nose.

"Whiskey isn't gonna save you," I snarl.

"But you… you said…" Yanni presses his lips into a thin line.

I grip Yanni's shoulders to pull him toward me, and at the same time, knee him in the groin. "I've wanted to do that for so long," I sneer close to his ear. "And the best part? I'm only getting started."

I shove Yanni to the floor and look at Malachi. "Do your worst."

Malachi claps his hands together like a giddy child. I move to stand by the wall so I can watch. Yanni scrambles to his knees and tries to crawl away from my cousin, playing his part perfectly.

Malachi kicks Yanni in the gut, and his arms give out. While he's laid out on the floor, Mal kicks him over and over. The sound of bone cracking reminds me of when Harlow fractured Peppermint's cheek, and my anger burns that much hotter.

"Don't kill him," I warn.

Malachi bends down and grabs Yanni by his shirt to lift him up a little. "I won't. But he'll wish I had, won't he?"

"I'll make sure of it."

Malachi reaches behind his back to grab his gun and presses the barrel to Yanni's forehead. "Tell me, old man. Why does my cousin want you dead more than he wants air to breathe?"

Yanni's eyes dart to me. "I-I don't know."

"Really, Yanni?" I narrow my eyes. "I think you do. Go ahead, it's okay. Tell him. Tell Malachi what he wants to know."

Yanni vehemently shakes his head. "He's crazy, Malachi. Blames me for being sent away. I swear, that's all. I didn't do anything."

Malachi laughs. "I'm not buying it."

"I'm not selling anything!" Yanni shouts. "I swe—"

"Take him to the bedroom," I demand. "It's my turn."

Malachi doesn't hesitate. He stands with Yanni in his grip and drags him to the only bedroom in the place. Yanni pleads with him to stop, to let him go, but Malachi ignores every word.

I open my bag and take out what I need, then follow. "Face down on the bed," I say when I enter the room.

Malachi throws Yanni to the mattress and, with a knee in his back, holds him still while I tie rope around his wrists and ankles, anchoring him to the metal bed frame. When Yanni is spread eagle and secure, Malachi backs up to the wall and lets me do my thing.

I drop the whip I brought to the floor and tighten my grip

on the sledgehammer. I swing the tool at the wall, reveling in the way Yanni jerks against his restraints when the plaster gives way.

Laughter fills the room, maniacal and dark, drowning out Yanni's desperate pleas for his life. I don't even realize the laughter belongs to me until I open my mouth to speak.

"This is gonna hurt," I taunt a split second before I shove the handle up his ass.

Yanni screams like a little bitch. I pull the handle out, twisting and turning it, and shove it back in. Blood coats the splintering wood, but still, I don't stop.

"This is for every motel room, every forced shower, every second of pain you caused me, every goddamn night I was trapped in hell with you." I shove it in one last time, all the way until the metal head of the sledgehammer rests against his ass cheeks. "That, you sick son of a bitch, is for Peppermint."

Leaving the hammer in place, I turn to get my whip, and Malachi's face catches my attention. He's staring at me, eyes wide, jaw dropped.

"What?"

He shakes his head. "Fuck, Nico. I didn't know."

I see things have clicked into place for him. "No one did."

We stare at one another for a moment, both of us trying to process the past and the present. I have one more secret, and it's time it was brought out into the light. I yank my shirt over my head and toss it to the floor.

I grab my whip and secure it in my grasp before turning back to face Yanni. I'm not surprised by the sharp intake of breath behind me. My scars are a lot for anyone to take in.

"Do you remember what else you would do to me, Yanni?" I ask in as I step next to the bed. "Do you remember all the times you made me bleed, saying it would turn me into a man?"

Yanni doesn't say a word. For a split second, I wonder if

he passed out, but then he starts begging again. Begging for a life he doesn't have a right to, for a soul that has no hope of being saved.

I raise the whip and bring it down across his back. Angry slashes crisscross his flesh with each pass of the cutting leather. Yanni screams loud enough to wake the dead. Unfortunately for him, his screams won't keep him from dying.

When his back is a bloody mass of muscle and tissue, I throw the whip to the floor and grab the knife I took from Peppermint's nightstand before leaving this morning. I lean over Yanni and press the serrated blade to his throat.

"Any last words?"

Yanni, the pitiful excuse for a human, mumbles incoherently.

"This is also for Peppermint," I snarl. "Go to hell you fucking bastard."

I increase the pressure and drag the blade across his neck, stealing his last breath. Standing up straight, I wipe the knife clean on my jeans. On autopilot, I pick up my whip and shirt. I don't look at Malachi as I stroll out of the room to grab my bag. I tuck the whip inside and put my shirt back on.

Malachi and I ignore the people standing in the hallway with fear in their eyes. They heard what just happened. I knew they would. I just didn't care.

When we reach the ground floor and head outside, Malachi stops in his tracks.

"Shit," he mutters and nods toward his car.

I follow his gaze and see a woman leaning against the back passenger door. Parked behind the vehicle is a Harley. The woman pushes away from the car and closes the distance between us.

"Malachi and Nico?"

"Who's asking?" I snap. She's not Peppermint or Harlow, so I don't feel particularly inclined to be friendly.

"Brazen," Malachi answers for her.

"You guessed it."

"Wait, Brazen as in the president of the DHMC mother chapter?"

"Your women called me. I gotta say, I don't think I've ever heard Harlow or Peppermint that angry." She focuses on Malachi. "Well, maybe Harlow. You did give her a run for her money a while back." Brazen takes a deep breath, sighs. "Look, I understand the need for vengeance, so this is your one pass. My cleanup crew will handle the apartment, I'll handle the neighbors and cops." She reaches out and grips both of our necks. "But if I ever catch you in my territory again, leaving a mess in your wake, Harlow and Peppermint will be planning funerals." She squeezes. "Got it?"

"Got it," we say in unison.

"Good. Now get the fuck outta here before I change my mind."

Brazen doesn't wait to see if we listen. Instead, she strolls inside the building like she owns the place.

"We are so fucked when we get home."

"You have no idea," Malachi agrees.

Malachi starts the car and pulls away from the curb.

"It's over, Nico," he says a few minutes later.

"It's just beginning."

CHAPTER 23

Peppermint

"I DON'T KNOW what more I can say."

My head is pounding so hard I'd swear on a stack of bibles that there's a full drumline in my skull. I rub my temples as I pace, but it does nothing to ease my suffering.

"There's nothing more to say," I tell Nico.

We've been fighting since he and Malachi returned from their field trip an hour ago. I don't know what's going on between Harlow and her husband, as she dragged him out of the clubhouse within minutes of their arrival. But if I know her as well as I think I do, no doubt they're argument is ten times worse than ours.

"I know you're mad," Nico says. "But I did what I had to do, and I won't apologize for it."

I whirl on him, stabbing a finger at his chest. "Mad? You think I'm mad?" I laugh bitterly. "I'm not mad, Nico. No. I'm fucking furious!"

"What do you want from me?" he asks calmly, which only ignites my fury more.

"I *want* you to not have gone without me. I *want* you to not have lied. I *want* a lot of things." I take a deep breath. "But it isn't about what I want, Nico. It's about what I need."

"What do you need?"

My anger deflates. He's too little, too late. And I'm not angry about that. I'm sad.

"I need a partner," I whisper brokenly. "I need the man in my life to treat me as his equal. I've been made to feel like I'm less than by my parents. I don't need it from you too."

I storm out of the room and down the stairs. Nico's footsteps thud behind me, but I ignore them, ignore him. I head outside and straight to my Harley. I need to get out of here, away from him.

"Don't do this, *cuore mio*," Nico pleads. "Don't walk away."

"I'm going to stay with Harlow and Malachi for a while."

I fire up my bike and ride away. I let the wind dry my tears and pray it can heal my soul. As I ride around absently, Nico's face flashes. I see him smiling and laughing. I see him angry and hurt. It's the hurt that sticks with me, the hurt that, in turn, hurts me.

Two hours later I knock on Harlow's front door. Within seconds, she's there pulling me in for a hug. We stand in the doorway for what feels like hours but is only minutes. Harlow lets me cry it out.

"C'mon, Pep." She pulls me inside and closes the door. "I take it things didn't go well?"

"They went as well as you'd expect. We fought, he refused to apologize, I left."

"Well, you know you're welcome here for as long as you need."

"Thanks. I know I could've stayed at the clubhouse, but I don't need everyone's pity. This just feels…" I shrug. "Safer I guess."

"I get it."

I look around the living room. "Where's Malachi? You didn't kill him, did you?"

Harlow's face hardens. "No, the fucker is still breathing. But I sent him to your place. I couldn't look at him." She rolls her eyes. "I told him he could come back in the morning, but that for now, I needed space."

"I'm sorry."

"For what?"

"You and Malachi should be enjoying your honeymoon, not sleeping in separate houses because of mine and Nico's demons."

"Pep, nobody in this family faces their demons alone. Ever."

"Still…"

"Stop it." Harlow urges me toward the couch. "Sit. I'll get us some ice cream and we can watch movies or something. Get our minds off reality for a while."

"Yeah, okay. That sounds good."

"It's ice cream and movies. Of course it sounds good."

———

Nico

The gaslight on the dash comes on just as I turn onto my road. I had over half a tank when I left the clubhouse, but I've been driving around for hours, not wanting to come home to an empty house.

As I get closer to the house, I see a car parked in the driveway. It takes a minute for it to register as Malachi's.

"Where the hell have you been?" he demands after I park and get out of the car.

"Driving around." I shrug. "Didn't wanna come home."

"I've been sitting here forever," he complains.

"Don't know what to tell you. Maybe try not letting your wife wear the pants in the family."

Pain radiates through my jaw when his fist plows into my face. He shifts to a fighting stance, but I only shake my head.

"Do whatever you want to me. I don't care anymore."

Malachi's shoulders slump. "She doesn't wear the pants. Not all the time anyway. And I can go home in the morning."

I chuckle, but there's no humor in it. "I'm happy for you. I'm pretty sure Peppermint will never speak to me again."

"I take it she's at my place?"

"Yep," I confirm.

I unlock the front door and quickly disarm the security system. After locking the door behind us, I stride to the kitchen.

"Wanna drink?" I ask as I retrieve a bottle of Jim Beam from the cabinet.

"Make it a double."

I pour our drinks and we retreat to the couch. I switch on the television and flip through the channels until I find a news station. I doubt we'll see anything about it on the local news, but curiosity has me wondering if Brazen was really able to clean up our mess.

"You're gonna have to fix this, Nico."

"Not sure it's fixable."

"It better be. I love Peppermint, but I don't exactly want to share my home with a third wheel so early in my marriage."

"Fuck, what does everyone want from me? Maybe I should go back to Seattle. Things were simpler then."

"Quit feeling sorry for yourself," Malachi snaps. "Couples fight. It happens. And then the man apologizes, and things return to normal."

"I'm not apologizing when I did nothing wrong."

"Ever heard the term 'happy wife, happy life'?"

"Peppermint's not my wife."

Malachi slaps me on the back.

"Relax. Everything will look better in the morning."

Malachi's a damn liar. Everything did not look better in the morning. Or the morning after that and the one after that. In fact, things couldn't get worse.

Or so I thought.

CHAPTER 24

Peppermint

TWO MONTHS LATER...

"THAT'S DISGUSTING."

I grin at Malachi before biting into the chocolate pudding covered pickle. I get a kick out of making him gag. It puts a smile on my face, even if it's superficial.

"Har, please kick her out," Malachi pleads as he bends over the trashcan. "She's making me sick."

Harlow carries her empty coffee mug to the sink and winks at me before addressing her husband. "Mal, she stays. But you can leave if it's too much."

He straightens quickly. "This is my house," he complains. "She has a perfectly good home to go to. I don't see why she has to stay here. Hell, she can even go to the clubhouse. I don't care."

I swallow my breakfast concoction. He's wrong. I don't have a home to go to. Not anymore. Nico and I only speak when it's absolutely necessary, which isn't often. He refuses to apologize, and I refuse to play second fiddle to his ego. We're both too stubborn for our own good.

"She's not going anywhere," Harlow says. "Not until she's ready."

Malachi groans and focuses on me now that my pickle is

gone. "Why won't you just talk to him? Nico knows he fucked up. He misses you."

"Is he sorry?"

"I give up." Malachi throws his hands up and stomps out of the kitchen.

Harlow starts washing the few dishes in the sink, and I dry them. We work in silence, but when I put the last mug away, that changes.

"Malachi's right, ya know?"

I glare at her. "About?"

"Pep, stop. This is getting ridiculous."

"Are you seriously siding with Nico?" I ask feeling betrayed.

"No, P, I'm not." She rests her hands on my slightly rounded belly. "I'm siding with him."

"I never should have told you it was a boy," I huff out.

Harlow laughs. "You didn't tell me. I had to bribe you with pickles for the information."

"Whatever."

"Look, all I'm saying is that Nico isn't going anywhere. He's the baby daddy. Even if you can't make it work between the two of you, he doesn't deserve to be cut out of that."

Tears well in my eyes. My cravings aren't the only thing all over the place. My emotions are too.

"I miss him," I admit.

"Then go talk to him."

"I can't."

"Why not?"

"Because."

"P, why?"

"Because I know if I talk to him, I'll forgive him."

"And that's a bad thing because…"

"He should be the one to cave first."

"In a perfect world, yes. But we don't live in a perfect world."

I sniffle and hiccup. "I don't even know what to say to him."

"How about you start with 'hi' or 'I miss you'?"

God, I want to. I want to go home and see Nico, move past whatever this is and get back to normal. Hell, I'd settle for a text from him. But he stopped sending those after the first week. I think it had to do with me threatening to keep the baby from him if he didn't stop, but that's beside the point. A pregnant woman can't be held responsible for her outbursts.

Can she?

"Go and talk to him," Harlow demands. "If you can't resolve things, then you can come back."

"Promise?"

"Yeah, P, I promise."

I nod and grab my cell off the table to send him a text. I'm not ready to go to the house and talk to him, but that doesn't mean we can't meet somewhere.

Me: Meet me at the clubhouse to talk?

I hit send. Seconds later, his response pops up.

Nico: Yes! When?

Me: Two hours?

Nico: See ya then.

"Is he willing to talk?" Harlow asks.

"I'm meeting him in two hours." For the first time in two months, I'm hopeful. But that sizzles as a new worry creeps in. "Shit."

"What?"

"What the fuck am I gonna wear?"

An hour and a half later I'm walking through the clubhouse and upstairs to my room. The only thing left here is the bed and nightstand. All of my other belongings were moved to the house I shared with Nico or Harlow and Malachi's, much to Mal's chagrin.

While I wait for Nico to arrive, I pace. I pace, and I think. What am I going to say to him? Is he going to apologize? Can we really work this out? My mind races with questions that I can't answer.

But I know what I want the answers to be. And somehow, that makes the wait more nerve-wracking because what if the answers I want aren't the ones I get?

Don't think like that.

I glance at my phone to check the time. There's still ten minutes to go so I go check myself out in the bathroom, making sure that my makeup still looks good. I didn't dress up or anything, but I did do what I could to look as good as possible.

My jeans hug my legs, and the long-sleeved tee I'm wearing under my cut stretches to accommodate my small baby bump. I run my fingers through my hair to fluff it up, and when I'm satisfied, I go sit on the bed.

And wait.

And wait some more.

I make a conscious effort not to check the time, but my phone pings with a notification.

Nico: I'm here. Can we talk outside? If Vinnie's attitude is anything to go by, I won't exactly be welcome in the clubhouse.

I roll my eyes and make a mental note to tell Vinnie to mind her own damn business. As I head downstairs, I type a quick text.

Me: Coming out

When I open the door, I spot Nico's car immediately. But it's not his car I want to see, it's him.

Damn tinted windows.

I walk around to the passenger side and climb in. I wait for him to say something, anything, but all he does is back away from the clubhouse and start toward the gate.

"We don't have to go anywhere," I tell him.

"I know," he responds, his eyes focused in front of him.

I shrug, not really giving a damn. We can talk anywhere.

"So…"

Why is this awkward? Even when I wasn't Nico's biggest fan, things between us were never awkward. My heart sinks. Is this what we've been reduced to? Awkward silences and one- or two-word responses?

"Where are we headed?"

"Someplace special."

"Can I get a hint?"

"Patience, Pepper."

"Pepper?" I swivel in my seat to stare at him. "Since when do you call me Pepper?"

It's my given name, but Nico's never used it, not even when he's trying to get under my skin.

Nico slams his hand into the steering wheel. "Dammit," he barks as he turns his head to finally look at me.

Motherfucking son of a whoring bitch-face twat.

The eyes. The eyes will give him away every single time. Why couldn't he have shown me his eyes when I got in the car?

"Hello Nicholi."

CHAPTER 25
Nico

I BREAK every speed limit to get to the clubhouse. I would've been on time, but my fucking car had a flat, so I had to change the tire. Then I had to take another shower to wash the grime away. I sent Peppermint a text to let her know I was running late, but she didn't respond. I can only hope this doesn't get added to her list of reasons to hate me.

I slam on the brakes at the gate and roll the window down.

"Hey Vinnie."

"Nico?" She steps up to the window and bends to peer in. "Where's Peppermint?"

"I'm meeting her here, and I'm running late, so if you could buzz me in, that'd—"

"You didn't have the spare tire on earlier," she comments as she looks toward the back tire I had to replace.

My blood runs cold.

"What do you mean 'earlier'? I wasn't here earlier."

No. This can't be happening.

Vinnie bends back down and locks eyes with me. "Shit."

"Vinnie?"

"His eyes are darker; they don't have the tiny gold flecks like yours."

"Vinnie?"

"I think Nicholi came out of hiding."

"Nicholi's here?"

"Uh, no. He left about twenty minutes ago. Peppermint was with him."

I stomp on the gas and send the car crashing through the gate. Metal screeches against metal. I call Peppermint's phone, but it goes straight to voicemail. Either it's dead, or Nicholi turned it off and ditched it.

I yank the steering wheel to the left to slide the car into a stop next to the clubhouse. Without bothering to cut the engine, I jump out and race inside.

"Story!"

I run upstairs and check Peppermint's room, hoping like hell that Vinnie was just messing with me. The room is empty.

"Story!" I shout again.

"What?" she barks when we almost collide on the staircase. "What's wrong?"

"Nicholi has Peppermint."

"What?"

We both go back downstairs. I follow her to the meeting room. There are two laptops open and running, along with scattered files and papers, on the table.

"Nico, he can't have her. There's been nothing to indicate that he's out of hiding."

"He has her, trust me."

"Where would he take her?" she asks as she sits and starts tapping the keyboard. "Any ideas?"

"I don't know."

"Think, Nico. There has to be a place that would mean something to him."

Nothing is coming to me. I hit the speed dial for Malachi and set my cell on the table.

"Nico, I have a meeti—"

"Nicholi has Peppermint," I bark.

"What?"

"He has her, Mal."

"How?"

"Harlow will have to ask Vinnie about that," I snap. "Get to the clubhouse and bring your wife. We need to find Peppermint."

"Yeah, okay. We'll be there."

"Wait," I shout before he can disconnect the call. "Any idea where he'd take her? Anything that jumps out at you?"

"No."

"Think, Mal," I demand. "You've been in the city your entire life. I haven't."

"And you kept tabs on the family the entire time you were gone. Start there."

Malachi disconnects the call, and I snag my cell off the table and throw it at the wall. When it shatters, I let out a primal howl.

"Here."

I glance at Story and stare at the cell phone she's handing to me.

"What?"

"Take it. I'll clone your number on it just in case she calls. You can buy me a new one when this is over."

I take the device and grip it in my hand like I need it to survive. "Thanks."

"Don't mention it." She focuses back on her laptop. "Malachi said to start with the information you had on the family. Do I have all of that?"

"I shared everything with you when we started tracking him last year."

"Everything?"

"Yes." I gasp. "Wait. No." I remove the flash drive that I keep on my key ring and hand it to her. "Here. There are a few files that I kept back."

Story eyes me skeptically but doesn't say anything. She plugs the drive in and gets to work. I, on the other hand, pace and try not to have a fucking heart attack.

———

Peppermint

"Where are we going?" I ask Nicholi for the hundredth time.

"You never quit, do you?"

"What? You thought I was going to make this easy on you?"

He smirks at me. "You're tied up. I'd say things have been pretty easy so far."

Asshole.

The only reason I'm bound in the backseat is because I tried to yank the wheel and cause him to wreck. He pulled over on the deserted road we'd been on and proceeded to tie me up. Oh, but being the gentleman he is, he gave me the option between duct tape over my mouth in the trunk or rope around my wrists and ankles in the backseat. I chose the backseat so I'd still have my voice.

I can still scream. If we ever get somewhere there's other people. As it is now, we're so far away from civilization that I wonder if I'd have been better off in the trunk.

No. I would've worn myself out trying to get out of the trunk. And what the hell would I have done if I'd gotten the stupid thing open? It's not like I could jump. Not without risking the baby. It irks me that I can't do what I would normally do and fight like hell, but it is what it is.

"Just tell me," I say. "It's not like it matters if I know."

"Shut up," he snaps.

"I'd rather talk. I hate silence. It's so boring."

Jesus, P. Quit antagonizing.

Nicholi grunts but doesn't respond otherwise. And I decide to be quiet, at least for a while. Talking is getting me nowhere. Besides, I need to come up with a plan, not trade insults and idle chit chat with my kidnapper.

When Nicholi stops the car about an hour later, I'm no closer to a plan than I was when I shut up. All I can think about is Nico and the baby, about how much time was wasted over the last two months. And for what? So I could keep my stubborn pride intact?

"We're here."

Nicholi cuts the engine and then steps out to open the back door. He drags me out and tosses me to the ground. Air whooshes from my lungs.

"Get up."

"If you want me up, why'd you throw me down?"

Nicholi leans over and backhands me across the face. "Get the fuck up."

I try, I really do, but it's hard to stand with your hands and feet bound. He watches me struggle for a few minutes before cutting the rope at my feet. With them loose, I'm able to stand.

I take in our surroundings, turning in circles to make sense of where we are. It appears to be an abandoned warehouse—such a cliché—encircled with a tall fence. It looks familiar, but I don't know why.

Nicholi drags me across the dead grass, through a hole in the fencing, toward the building.

"I really tried to get it right."

"Get what right?"

"You'll see."

He leads me inside the building, then through a hallway to the left. When we reach the end, he shoves open a door and we go down a concrete staircase. The lower we go, the colder it gets, and the more trepidation fills me.

At the bottom of the steps, Nicholi flips a switch. The large space is awash in fluorescent lighting, and every muscle in my body tenses.

"Welcome home, Pepper."

CHAPTER 26

Nico

"I NEED YOU TO STOP PACING."

I glower at Story. I've been helping her as much as possible, but the day is almost over, and we still have nothing.

"I can't. It helps me think."

"Yeah, well it distracts me."

"Too damn bad."

"Both of you," Harlow snaps. "Stop. You two arguing isn't going to find my VP."

Story shakes her head but gets back to work. I, on the other hand, stalk to the window to look outside. The sun went down a while ago, which means the temperature did too.

Is Peppermint okay? Is she cold? Is she hurt? Fuck, is she alive?

"She's alive," I mutter to myself. "I'd know it if she weren't."

A hand rests on my shoulder. "Yeah, you'd know it," Harlow says. "And so would I."

I rest my forehead against the glass. "What if she's hurt?"

"If she's hurt, she'll heal," Harlow insists. "Pep is so much stronger than you give her credit for."

"I've always thought she was strong. I just hated that she felt like she always had to be."

"Nico, you need to pull yourself together. Can you do that?" Harlow's voice cracks. "For me? Please?"

I turn and pull Harlow into my chest. Just like Peppermint, she shouldn't always have to be strong.

"We'll get her back," she says into my shirt.

"Lucky for you, I know you're in love with someone else."

Harlow and I break apart and face Malachi. "And you know I love you," she says to him.

"I know, *bella*."

A fist of jealousy wraps around my heart. Fuck, I need Peppermint.

"Any news from Coast?" I ask.

"His entire club is out searching. Fiona and a few of the others are with them. They'll call if they find anything."

"Right."

"Hey, Harlow?"

We all turn to Story.

"Did you find her?" Harlow asks.

"No but come look at this." Harlow moves to stand behind Story and look over her shoulder. "Does that look familiar?"

"Yeah." She shakes her head. "But I don't know why. Put it up for the guys to see."

With a few clicks of her mouse, Story has her laptop screen projected onto the wall.

"It's the old warehouse."

"What warehouse?" Harlow asks.

"Back before the beef between our families, my father procured two warehouses," Malachi begins. "One of them was destroyed after your mom was killed. But this one…"

"It's sat empty and unused since then," I add.

"Are they identical?" Story asks.

"Yeah. The same company owned them before going bankrupt. That's when the Ricci's bought them."

"Okay, so that explains why it looks familiar," Story says absently. "It matches the building where Velvet was killed, and we have all of the schematics in our club records. I must have seen it when I started digitizing everything and it stuck in my mind for some reason."

"Could he have taken Peppermint there?" Harlow asks.

I look at Malachi and he nods. Good, we're both on the same page.

"Yeah," I tell them. "After we took out the Family last year, Malachi and I sold the building. Some corporation bought it. Said they were going to demolish it and build condos or something."

"And you didn't dig into the corporation's background?"

"Not too much. Everything was on the up and up."

"We both just wanted rid of it," Malachi says.

"Well, the building sold again, about two months later. It's now owned by another corporation. Which isn't a corporation at all, but shell company after shell company after shell company." Story pulls up another tab. "The man in the center of it all? Craig Moore. Only Nico, you were Craig Moore, so it stands to reason that it's Nicholi."

"Son of a bitch!"

"Story, can you see if any modifications have been made since he bought it?"

"Yeah." She starts to type again. "What are you thinking?"

"The other building, the one that was destroyed had tunnels beneath it. That's where he kept his *product*." Malachi sneers the word. "That's where Peppermint would have been. If Nicholi took her to this other building, I'm guessing he's keeping her underground. He wouldn't risk staying in the building itself. He's been planning this for too long to make a rookie mistake like that."

"Oh my God. He's recreating the last time they were together, back when she was fifteen." Harlow's face falls.

"There are tunnels," Story confirms. "But I don't think they're original to the property." She brings up yet another tab. "There's been numerous deliveries to the property, all in the name of Craig Moore. Concrete, lumber, rebar, chains. Nicholi is recreating things for sure, right down to the last detail."

"Story, send the address to everyone's cell phone and tell them to come ready for war," Harlow instructs as she back-steps toward the door. "Nico, Malachi, unless you want me to leave without you, I suggest you pick up your fucking feet and move."

Orders issued, she turns and runs out of the clubhouse. Malachi and I race after her, jumping in his car while she's on her Harley. I've never been more grateful for Malachi's expensive taste in fast cars as I am now.

"She knows where she's going?" I ask as I grab on to the handle above the door when he takes a sharp turn.

"Story would've sent the address to her too. Her Bluetooth will read it to her and feed her the directions."

"Right."

As Malachi drives at speeds that would put a race car driver to shame, I pray. I haven't prayed since I was a little boy, before my father killed my mother, but I'm hoping that whatever deity is out there forgives me for that. Because I need them to answer my prayers.

Hang on, cuore mio. I'm coming for you.

You better run, Nicholi. I'm gunning for you.

CHAPTER 27

Peppermint

"I HAVE BEEN DREAMING of this since I was thirteen."

"You've been dreaming about raping me in a makeshift cage on a concrete floor?" I shake my head. "You don't aim high, do you?"

Nicholi digs his fingers into my thigh. He ripped my clothes off me before he chained me to the floor. Smoke is still curling out of the pipe attached to the top of the small incinerator on the other side of the bars. I can handle being naked and chained. Hell, it's not like it's the first time. But burning my cut is another matter.

"Ya know, I was glad when Nico pussied out back then," Nicholi says conversationally. He runs his hand up and down my thigh as he speaks, and I fight like hell not to react. "The thought of him touching you, of fucking you…" He shudders. "I wanted you from the moment Yanni brought you back from his hunting trip." Nicholi laughs. "That's what we used to call it. A hunting trip. Because he would hunt for victims."

"Yeah, got it. Don't care."

Blood pools on my tongue when he backhands me.

"I was so angry when Yanni showed up that day. Don't get me wrong, I'm glad he did. Otherwise, that biker bitch probably woulda killed me. But he showed up and then you were gone."

Nicholi shifts to lean against the iron bars on the opposite side of the cage.

"After you, things were never the same. Nico was sent away, which at the time, I was happy about it, but then I realized that he got what he wanted. He hated being a Ricci. But me? All I wanted was you."

"Sucks to be you."

"It did. But now?" He leers at me, stares at my tits with a glint in his eye. "It's not so bad. Especially now that Father and Uncle are gone. I don't have to answer to them anymore. I don't have to pretend that I give a damn about human trafficking or money or any of that shit."

Nicholi shifts to his knees and crawls closer. "But do you want to know what I do give a damn about?"

"Not really."

He reaches out and pinches my nipple. He pinches and pulls and does his best to inflict pain. And it's working. But he doesn't need to know that.

"I give a damn about you." Nicholi moves his hand to my stomach. "I'm not crazy about this, but I'll deal."

I try to kick out, but the chains cuffed to my ankle are too short.

"You won't get away with this," I snarl. "Nico will find me."

"Will he?"

That's the million-dollar question.

"Okay, fine." He sighs. "Let's say Nico finds you. Then what?"

"I can think of a few things."

"I'm sure you can. But if you're thinking he's going to kill me, think again. Although…"

I avert my eyes, unable to look at him any longer. The only time I want to see that particular face is when it's Nico.

"Maybe Nico will kill me." Nicholi starts to pace the confined space. "Not really, but that's what we can make the world think, right? We are twins."

"No one who knows Nico would ever mistake you for him."

"You did."

I whip my head around and glare at him.

"Oh, don't get so upset. It's not good for the baby."

I struggle against the chains, yanking and pulling as hard as I can, knowing it's futile but having to do something. Nicholi simply stands there and watches me with a bored expression on his goddamn smug face.

Sweat coats my skin, blood seeps from the wounds created by my shackles, and still I struggle.

"Do your fucking worst, you sick fuck," I snarl. "You think killing Nico is the way to win me over? Then go ahead and try. See where that gets you."

"It'll get me you."

"Maybe in the flesh," I concede. "But that's it. My heart and my soul does, and will always, belong to Nico."

Nicholi lunges forward and drops to straddle my hips. I turn my head to the side, but he grips my chin and forces me to look at him.

"You are going to watch me while I take you," he snarls.

He uses his free hand to undo his pants and then rises up to push them down over his hips. His flaccid dick flops out.

"I thought you said you were gonna take me," I taunt, which earns me another backhanded slap. I lick the blood off my lip. "Kinda hard to… shit, sorry. It's not hard."

"You smart-mouthed bitch," he roars as he thrusts his hips forward until his cock head is pressed against my lips. Nicholi grips my jaw to force my mouth open. "Hard to talk like this, isn't it?"

Fair point. It is. But…

I bite down as hard as I can. Nicholi tries to yank free, but my teeth hang on.

Hard to get a boner with a broke wanker, isn't it?

Nicholi pummels my face until I release him, then scrambles off me to the opposite side again. I turn my head and spit out blood and whatever else I managed to rip off him.

"Psycho cunt," he rages.

"Not exactly what you were hoping for, am I?"

"You're everything I've ever wanted!" he shouts.

Nicholi stands, but when he tries to take a step, he stumbles with his pants half off. He yanks them up, hissing when the material grazes his torn flesh.

"I've done everything right. I played the game, bided my time... You're mine!" Nicholi paces, and I keep my eyes on him. "Nico should have stayed away. But no, once again, he's getting the life he wants. My fucking life!"

"Do you even hear yourself?" I ask. "Nothing you say makes sense. Nothing you do makes sense. If you wanted me, what were the others for? What purpose did Bethany serve? Or Tasha? They didn't have to die."

"Yes they did," he roars. "They weren't you!"

All I can do is stare. There is no reasoning with the unreasonable. And Nicholi is beyond unreasonable. He's certifiable. In every way. I bet if he were evaluated, loads of issues would be discovered. Maybe his childhood fucked him up. Maybe it was not having a mother. Maybe his mind just cracked one day and never sealed back up.

Who the fuck knows?

Whatever it is in him that's broken isn't going to get resolved in time to save me. I'm not going to be able to talk my way out of this.

Nico, where are you? I know I'm stubborn, and I know I told you I can take care of myself, but this time, I can't. I need you. Our baby boy needs you.

Nicholi stands over me and presses a booted foot into my

chest to hold me down. His stare is crazed, and fear settles in my gut. I've managed to keep it at bay up until now.

"Maybe I can't fuck you, but that doesn't mean I can't take what's mine." He lowers himself over me to straddle my hips again. I buck wildly, but that only makes him laugh. "Struggle, please. I like a little fight."

Nicholi leans forward and licks a nipple before biting down. Then he repeats the process on the other side. Tears well in my eyes because there's nothing I can do to stop him. I'm trapped, destined to be raped by this man.

I close my eyes and rely on an old trick. I force myself to go somewhere else in my mind.

Waves crash against the sand, the white caps beautiful. Nico's there, and so is our son. They're walking toward me, father and toddler, hand in hand. I run to them, pumping my legs until, but the faster I run, the greater the distance between us.

Nico!

I call out to him, over and over, screaming at the top of my lungs for him to stop, to wait for me, but I don't think he hears me.

Nico, please!

"Stop fighting me."

"I'll never stop," I sob.

"Stop, *cuore mio*. It's me. I'm right here."

My eyes fly open and I'm staring into dark orbs that seem to see right through to my soul. The eyes. The eyes tell me everything.

"Nico?"

When the man above me nods, the fluorescent light catches the gold flecks.

Chains prevent me from throwing my arms around him. I keep trying, ignoring the pain and the blood.

"P, stop!"

I whip my head to the side and see Harlow standing there.

She's gripping her hatchet, but there's no blood on the blade. She must not have used it.

"Where's Nicholi?" I ask, frantically searching for him.

"Malachi has him upstairs," Nico tells me.

Harlow starts to work on the cuffs, muttering the entire time about needing me to teach her to lockpick. I'd laugh at her if the situation wasn't so fucked up.

"Is he dead?" I ask.

Nico shakes his head. "No."

"He's mine," I snarl, some of my fight returning.

Harlow gets me free, and Nico helps me stand. He shrugs off his jacket and puts it on me. Fortunately, he's a tall man so it hangs almost to my knees.

"Where's your cut?" Harlow asks.

I nod toward the incinerator.

"You've got to be fucking kidding me."

"Nope."

"Pep, we end this. Now."

She storms toward the stairs, but Nico holds me in place.

"You're coming home."

I cup his cheek. "Yes, I am."

Nico nods, then links his fingers with mine to lead me up the steps. When we reach the expanse of the warehouse's main level, I'm shocked at what I see. DHMC members, Coast's club members, and Forza Security employees are forming a giant circle. Every single person is holding a weapon, and their death stares are trained on Nicholi, who's tied to a metal chair in the middle.

Coast and Fiona are the closest to me, and they step aside to allow me, Nico, Malachi, and Harlow into the circle to face the enemy. Nicholi is naked, just like I was, and his dick is barely hanging on.

"I see someone took things a step further than I did," I comment.

"That was me," Spooks pipes up from her position. "I

couldn't let you have all the fun."

I laugh at her, feeling lighter than I have in years.

"Pep, this is your show, your call," Harlow says. "What happens to him?"

"Oh, he dies here. But I think I'll let the three of you get in a few licks first."

Malachi doesn't hesitate. He points his gun at Nicholi's right knee and pulls the trigger. Then he does the same to the left. Nicholi howls in pain, but if thinks he's hurting now, he's sadly mistaken.

"Next," I say.

Harlow grips the handle of her custom hatchet and swings it at Nicholi's right arm, severing it from his body. Blood gushes from the stump to pool around him. Harlow steps back.

"Only one arm?" I question.

Harlow shrugs. "Less blood loss. You get his death."

I nod.

"Next."

Nico holds his 9mm in one hand and a knife in the other. But rather than use either of them against Nicholi, he turns to face me, and then drops them both on the floor.

"Nico?"

"This one's for you. I won't take any more of his pain away from you."

How did I get so lucky?

I slowly walk toward Nicholi. His head lolls to the side, but he's alive. Barely. I crouch in front of him.

"Not so tough now, are ya?"

He tries to open his mouth to speak, but he's too weak.

"It's okay. There's nothing left to say really." I stand and press my blade against his throat. "Well, nothing but fuck you, piss off, and good riddance."

I slit Nicholi's throat and watch the life drain from the evil twin's eyes.

Epilogue

NICO

Eight months later…

"YOU KNOW I don't like surprises."

I hold the blindfold in place over my wife's eyes and hope I'm not making a huge mistake. I'm fairly certain I'm not, but with this family, one can never be completely sure.

"I know you don't."

"Then why are you surprising me?" she grumbles. "And why couldn't Nicholas come with us?"

Nicholas Craig Ricci was born a few weeks early via natural childbirth. I tried to convince Peppermint to have an epidural, but she insisted that she could handle the pain. As soon as she was done pushing and Nicholas was handed to her, she made me promise to give her the drugs next time.

"Because some things aren't appropriate for babies."

"If he's with his mommy and daddy, it's appropriate."

"Do you remember the first time we had sex?"

"Uh, yeah. Not sure what that has to do with anything."

"If Nicholas would have been in the room, would that have been appropriate?"

"Of course not."

"Then not everything involving mommy and daddy is appropriate."

"Fuck you."

I nip at her ear. "Later, I promise."

The door in front of us opens, and I guide Peppermint into the meeting room at the clubhouse. I wanted to do this at home, but the internet connection is better here. At least, that's what Story said. Judging by the lined walls of DHMC members, I think she had another agenda.

My eyes land on Harlow, who's holding our sleeping son, and she winks. Ah, so this was her doing. It's probably better this way, to be honest. The more people she has in her corner, the better.

"Okay, we're here."

Peppermint's hands fly to the blindfold, but I catch them in my own and move to stand in front of her.

"Not yet." When she opens her mouth to argue, I kiss her. I can feel the eye-rolling of the others around us. "Do you trust me?"

"I thought I did. I'm having second thoughts."

"Be serious," I chide.

"When am I not serious?"

Several snorts sound around the room, and Peppermint stomps her foot in annoyance.

"Who else is here?" she demands. "Nico, what the hell is going on?"

I glare at them, but then shake my head and decide to go with it. I should know by now that planning anything with this group is pointless. I lift the blindfold and turn my wife in a circle so she can see them all.

"Now I'm worried," she says. "Is something wrong?" Her

eyes land on Harlow, which means she spots her son. "Hand him over, Har."

Harlow does, and Peppermint snuggles Nicholas into her chest. "Mommy's got you, little nugget."

Yes, the nickname somehow stuck.

"Auntie Har had him just fine," Harlow huffs.

"*Bella*, stop," Malachi teases as he pulls his wife back into his arms. "Our nugget will be here before you know it." He rubs her very pregnant belly as if to prove his point.

"Anyway, back to the surprise." I kiss the top of Nicholas's head and then my wife on the lips. "I have someone I want you to meet," I tell her.

Peppermint glances around the room. "Okay, who?"

I look over my shoulder at Story, who's waiting patiently with her laptop. "Go ahead," I tell her.

Story's screen mirrors on the wall, and two people stare at us. I turn Peppermint to face them, and she gasps.

"Mr. and Mrs. Canton," I begin. "I'd like you to meet my wife, Pepper Ricci."

Mrs. Canton bristles. "What is the meaning of this?"

"What the fuck, Nico?" Peppermint cries.

"Language," Mr. Canton chastises, as if he's talking to his little girl and not the grown woman before him.

"Trust me," I tell my wife. When she nods, albeit with a look that promises revenge, I turn to face the screen. "I wanted to meet the daughter you tossed aside like garbage because of something that wasn't her fault. I wanted you to see the woman she's become, the wife and mother your little girl grew up to be."

"Our daughter died years ago," Mrs. Canton says.

"That's one thing we can agree on. Pepper Canton died at the hands of my family, my brother. We were the evil in that scenario, not her."

"What is your point?"

"My point, you crusty old bitch, is this," I snap, no longer willing to play nice with such horrid people. "Your daughter, the one you gave birth to and should have loved unconditionally, is absolutely, unequivocally dead. But this woman?" I point to Peppermint. "She was born the day your daughter died. She is the—"

"What my husband is trying to say," Peppermint begins sweetly. Too sweetly. "Is that your hatred of me didn't fuck me up. It might have knocked me down a peg or two, but I climbed my way out of hell, with a new family, and became someone better than you ever could have made me."

Peppermint sweeps her arm around the room. "These people are my family. They support me, love me, empower me every single day." She grabs my hand. "Nico is my husband. The brother of my worst nightmare, but the brightest part of my world." She kisses Nicholas on his head, and our son stirs awake. "This is my son, your biological grandson. He reminds me that there's still magic in the world, that even on my worst day, I'm worthy of love."

When she points to Harlow, Harlow moves to stand behind us, her hatchet raised above her head.

"She is my sister."

She points to Mama, Giggles, and Spooks. "They are my sisters," she says as they all move to stand behind us, blades raised above their heads.

This repeats, over and over, until every person in the room is standing behind our family of three, weapons raised.

"Shut this damn thing off," Mrs. Canton barks at her husband. "I don't deserve to be disrespected like this."

Peppermint very calmly hands Nicholas to me and then removes her knife from its sheath at her hip.

"It's okay, I'm almost done," she snarls and raises her knife like the others. "Take a good look, *Mom and Dad*." She sneers the titles. "Because *I* am what your DNA created. Now, if you'll excuse me, I have family shit to get back to." Peppermint starts to turn away from the screen but halts and looks back up at them. "Oh, and one more thing. Fuck. You."

Story cuts the feed, leaving Mr. and Mrs. Canton to sputter over their words and try to figure out what the hell just happened.

Peppermint faces me and grins. "I changed my mind."

"About?"

"I find that surprises aren't so bad."

Laughter fills the room, but Peppermint remains stone-cold sober. She raises onto her tiptoes and kisses me. When she breaks contact, she smiles.

"Thank you for this."

"I never want you to doubt your worth again. You should always be confident about how loved and appreciated you are, as a friend, as a wife, and as a mother. But most of all, I wanted you to see that there is not a single person in your life who thinks you're weak or that you can't take care of yourself."

"I'm guessing you're going to tell me that even though I can take care of myself, I shouldn't always have to."

"Exactly, *cuore mio*. You catch on quick."

Next in the Devil's Handmaidens MC Series

Mama's Rules: Book 3

Mama...

I don't have much in this world beyond The Devil's Handmaidens MC, and I've always been okay with that. My sisters are my life, our mission my reason for being. But that all changes when a little boy chooses me to be his protector, to be his voice.

When I take him home, my plan is to drop him off and get

out of dodge. Unfortunately, I'm met with a father who doesn't know how to drag himself out of the pits of Hell. And for some reason beyond my understanding, I want to help. I just have to convince the man, and my club, that I can.

But helping them isn't the only problem I'm facing. No, I also have to help stop the new threat to the club and community, all the while protecting the boy and the man I'm coming to regard as family.

Benson...

Losing my wife was the hardest thing I've ever had to deal with in my life. At least, until the day my son was kidnapped. When the police came up against dead end after dead end, I thought he was lost forever. My world became a black hole I couldn't escape from.

I drown myself in booze, every day trying to numb the pain of my new hellish existence. It never works, but my heart doesn't seem to care. That is, until a woman shows up on my doorstep, with my son in tow. I know I need to be the father my son deserves, but it's not easy. And it's made harder when the woman insists on helping because she makes me want more than to simply get better. She makes me want to be the man I thought was long dead.

When evil reappears, threatens to destroy the new life I'm building, can I keep those I love safe, or will the bad guys win again?

About the Author

Andi Rhodes is an author whose passion is creating romance from chaos in all her books! She writes MC (motorcycle club) romance with a generous helping of suspense and doesn't shy away from the more difficult topics. Her books can be triggering for some so consider yourself warned. Andi also ensures each book ends with the couple getting their HEA! Most importantly, Andi is living her real life HEA with her husband and their boxers.

For access to release info, updates, and exclusive content, be sure to sign up for Andi's newsletter at andirhodes.com.

Also by Andi Rhodes

Broken Rebel Brotherhood

Broken Souls

Broken Innocence

Broken Boundaries

Broken Rebel Brotherhood: Complete Series Box set

Broken Rebel Brotherhood: Next Generation

Broken Hearts

Broken Wings

Broken Mind

Bastards and Badges

Stark Revenge

Slade's Fall

Jett's Guard

Soulless Kings MC

Fender

Joker

Piston

Greaser

Riker

Trainwreck

Squirrel

Gibson

Satan's Legacy MC

Snow's Angel

Toga's Demons

Magic's Torment

Duck's Salvation

Dip's Flame

Devil's Handmaidens MC

Harlow's Gamble

Peppermint's Twist

Mama's Rules

Valhalla Rising MC

Viking

Mayhem Makers

Forever Savage

Printed in Great Britain
by Amazon